Don't Forget What Grandma Said!

By James L. Darby

YDarbPress Publishing Company

ISBN 978-0578405155

Cover illustrated by Alvin Smith at Urban Design Suite
Edited by Eryka Parker at Lyrical Innovations, LLC
Library of Congress Control Number: 2010 906997
YDarbPress Publishing, Cleveland Ohio 44120
ydarbpress@yahoo.com
Printed in the United States of America

Dedication

This book is dedicated to my wife, Monica
who has helped me make this a reality. Your
patience and understanding are worth more than
the finest gold.
You are truly my Darlin-Darlin Baby.

Acknowledgments

I would like to thank my wife and five children for their ongoing support. Thanks to my mom and dad for how you raised me. Thank you, Grandma Ray and Grandma Darby for being the women of God that you are. To my brothers Jermaine, Steve, and Joseph: my deepest gratitude. To my countless other family and friends: I thank you very much. Thank you, Greg Laury, for being my true friend who always told me I could make it. I love you so much. Thank you, Renee Thomas, for being a positive influence in my life. Your encouragement has helped me to reach greater heights. Thank you, Shawn "Big Time" Ray, my buddy since first grade. Thank you for always telling the truth about everything. To my Pastor, R. A. Vernon, and First Lady, Lady Vernon: thank you for speaking into my life on a weekly basis and challenging Monica and me to become better people in the Lord. I truly thank you for starting "The Word" Church, the best church in the world.

Table of Contents

Foreword

When James first announced that he would write and publish this book, everyone applauded his intentions. James wrote the key points of this book on the back of an old schedule from his job. He read it with such enthusiasm when he proclaimed, "The Lord gave me an idea for a book." It felt good watching him pen this book, a few lines at a time; sitting at the kitchen table, staring into space, and picking at the low-cut strands of his salt and pepper hair. He often asked, "What do you think about this?" I got a thrill when he would say, "check this out..." or "let me read this to you". I smiled every time a new character was introduced. God only knows where James got the character names, but it really seems like they could be close family or friends.

Even though Caleb is a fictional character, in many ways, he could be any of us. James and I often find ourselves saying, when we were kids, things were nothing like they are today. We laugh about not having the luxuries of going to restaurants. Wendy's was upscale dining for us. The troubles that young people face today are much different from our generation. I'm sure each generation feels the same. We often wonder what it will take to get their attention, many times wishing someone had spoken a word of wisdom prior to the mess we found ourselves in. Would we have heeded the warnings? I would like to think yes. When we talk with our children, we are desperately hoping they will listen to everything we say and somehow avoid the pitfalls of life. Funny thing, those life experiences, hurt, and disappointments make us who we are.

The real hero of the story is Grandma Lois. When making foolish mistakes, who, in hindsight, hasn't wished we had a Grandma Lois there to offer loving guidance, wisdom, and forgiveness? She expressed both love and compassion unconditionally. Her words of wisdom proved helpful in shaping Caleb into a strong man of God.

I truly believe this book can make a difference in your life. Whether you are a young person going into adolescence, a high school student on your way to college or an independent adult, it is my prayer that the wisdom Grandma Lois shares with Caleb impacts your life in a positive way.

Monica Darby
Loving Wife & Devoted Mother

Chapter One

"Caleb...Caleb...

*W*ake up!" I heard my father call. I looked at the clock. It was time to get up for school.

Once I got downstairs, my mom, busy finishing breakfast, gave me a kiss and said good morning.

"Morning, Mom," I responded.

"Your dad and I will have to use your car today. The other car is down, and I have a doctor's appointment. We're going to drop you off at school."

I nodded, slightly irritated at the idea of being dropped off by my parents as a high school senior. My text notification went off. I looked down at the screen.

What's up, C?

I text him back. *Ay Mark.*

Just wanted to remind you to bring the DVD.

I won't forget… As a matter of fact, can I roll with you to school today?

Yeah. Be there in 15.

I let my parents know I was catching a ride to school with Mark. As I put on my coat and grabbed my books, my mom said, "Don't forget to slide your house key off your key ring. You'll need it to get in if you ride back with Mark."

"All right."

"And the driveway needs to be shoveled when you get home today," my dad said, chiming in.

"All right," I replied.

"We'll be back around two, before you get out of school. Call us if you end up needing a ride back home," he added.

"Okay."

Shortly after, I heard Mark blowing his horn outside. Just as I headed out the door, my dad said to me, "Have a good and productive day in school and we love you, son."

Wow, I thought. That told me there was something on Dad's mind because he rarely told me he loved me. I started wondering about the details of Mom's appointment.

Mom, on the other hand, gave me her usual hug and kiss and said, "God bless you, Caleb. I love you and Jesus does too."

I glanced at my phone as I entered the school. I still had ten minutes before the bell rang, so I headed to my locker to grab the rest of my books. I heard someone calling me from the other side of the hallway and turned in time to see her smiling face.

"Morning, Caleb," said my classmate Yvonne.

"Oh hey, Yvonne. What's good?"

"Hey," she said, brushing her hair back from her face. "Did you study for the test?"

"Yeah. You?" I asked her. I wasn't totally comfortable with the material, but this wasn't something I would admit to Yvonne or anyone for that matter.

"A little bit." She shrugged her shoulders casually.

I nodded. "Okay, I see studying isn't a necessity for you."

She chuckled shyly. We continued the small talk until the bell rang.

"See you in class later." She gave a finger wave before walking away.

"Okay."

I walked through the classroom door and took my usual seat near the back of the room. While we were taking the practice test in Mr. Long's class, our assistant principal, Mr. Smith, walked in and asked for a word with our teacher. We all knew whatever his said couldn't be good. We rarely saw Mr. Smith. Once they left the classroom, we began making small talk and comparing our answers, taking full advantage of the break. Mr. Long's absence was very brief, but the pained expression on his face once he returned made us all stop in mid-sentence.

Mr. Long paused for a moment before laying his eyes on me. My heart stopped. "Caleb, can you please go with Mr. Smith to his office?"

I swallowed before asking, "Uhh... why, Mr. Long?"

"They need to see you down there," Mr. Long said, his eyes on the floor.

I gathered my things and left the room, which had grown silent. I looked at Mr. Long and, when he finally looked up, I read disappointment in his eyes.

It's just a practice test. Everyone was talking when he left the room. I wonder if I'm being singled out... I thought. *No, that's not it. Mr. Smith came in before that even happened. What's going on?*

As we made the long walk down the hallway to the administrative office, my pulse thumped loudly in my ears. I tried to think of reasons why I was called to the office. I hadn't been in any kind of trouble and my grades were fine.

When we finally arrived at the main office, the principal, Ms. Johnson and the school guidance counselor were standing by the door. They greeted me before Ms. Johnson escorted us to her office and shut the door behind us.

Ms. Johnson's tone was stern as she instructed, "Have a seat, Caleb."

My stomach was filled with fluttering butterflies as I wiped my sweaty palms on my khakis. I took a seat in front of her large oak desk then glanced over and noticed a police officer standing at the back of her office in a snug navy-blue uniform. His presence increased my nervousness and I really began to wonder what was going on. What kind of trouble could I possibly be in?

I said to him, "Sir, I haven't done anything wrong."

He nodded, then introduced himself as Officer Kominsky.

"Hi, I'm Caleb," I replied, offering a shaky hand, even though I was sure he already knew me. Although his smile appeared a little comforting and his grip was firm, I still felt anxious about why they called me down there in the first place.

He nodded. "Caleb. That's a biblical name."

My God. Kill the small talk! Why in the world am I here? I thought as I nodded numbly. "Yes, it is, sir."

"Caleb, I have some difficult news to share with you."

I nodded, just wanting him to spit it out. What in the world could I have done to demand all the theatrics?

He continued, "Your parents were involved in a bad car accident almost an hour ago."

My heart jumped into my throat and I immediately felt sick to my stomach. "Wha... what happened?"

He sighed before continuing. "As you know, the condition of the roads this morning was extremely icy and slick. Your parents were traveling through a snow belt. According to a couple of eyewitnesses, a deer pranced out in front of your car. When your father slammed on the brakes to avoid hitting it, the car spun out and eventually slammed head first into an empty tractor trailer parked on the side of the road. Your parents are both in critical condition at Hillcrest Hospital. We need to get you there as soon as possible."

I stared at him dumbfounded. What was he telling me? How in the world had this happened? I'd seen my parents less than an hour and a half ago and they were just fine. Maybe he was mistaken.

The school counselor stepped up to me and laid a hand on my right shoulder. "Caleb, I know this is some pretty shocking news to swallow. I understand you may be feeling a little confused right now. Just listen to Officer Kominsky so we can get you to the hospital as quickly as possible to see your parents. Okay?"

I finally turned and looked at her numbly for a moment, then over at Principal Johnson. I then realized that her stern look earlier wasn't a stern look at all. It was one of concern. Her eyes were soft as she looked at me and nodded in agreement with the counselor's advice. They were all watching me closely, so I swallowed and nodded that I understood.

"We ran the plates on the car and that's how we found you. We need to act fast, Caleb. Is there anyone you would like us to contact before we take you down there?"

I shook my head, trying to think clearly. "Uh... yes. Please call my Grandmother, Lois." I rattled off her telephone number. My mind raced, and I wondered about the severity of my parents' condition. I sat in the police vehicle, waiting for them to take me to the hospital. It was my first time inside a police car, but it wouldn't be my last.

When I got to the hospital, all I could hear was "Code blue, emergency room. Code blue, emergency room." As I walked into the waiting area, my Aunt Shirley and Uncle Cal ran up to me and gave me a hug.

Uncle Cal said, "It's going to be okay, Caleb."

How do you know that? You don't really know that! I thought, but I nodded anyway.

We sat in painful silence in the waiting room for almost an hour, watching the nurses and doctors scrambling frantically around halls. Then, I looked up to see my Grandma Lois burst through the doors. She smiled sadly at me and gave me one of her infamous bear hugs.

"I love you, my Caleb," she said, rubbing my back.

I sighed. "I love you too, Gram."

She acknowledged Cal and Shirley, then turned her attention back to me. "How are your mother and father?"

"I don't know yet. No one has been able to tell us what's going on with them. I'll find out." I walked over to the nurses' station. "Ma'am, can you please find out the status my parents, Eunice and David Farnsley? We don't know if they're still in surgery or not."

She nodded and began typing, but before she could give me an answer, a doctor walked soberly through the double doors asking, "Are you the family of David and Eunice Farnsley?"

"Yes," my grandmother said, clutching her chest.

My eyes were glued to the doctor's face and I couldn't move a bone in my body. I waited to hear what he had to tell us.

"Hello, I'm Doctor Roberts, the Head Trauma Specialist. Unfortunately, during the accident, both Eunice and David suffered severe head injuries. We attempted surgery, but I am very sorry to inform you that neither of them survived it."

Chapter Two

"Oh, Lord!" My Grandma's shout echoed throughout the corridor. As I sat there listening to the doctor, tears streamed down my face. I immediately turned to comfort her. I was devastated and trying to get my head around what the doctor had just told us. Did he really say my parents were dead? *Both* of them? Where did that leave me? Did that make me an orphan? Where was I going to live?

Grandma hugged me tightly and said, "Caleb, your mom and dad have passed away and I'm so sorry! They've gone home to be with the Lord. But you will see them again, Caleb. Just trust in the Lord."

"Grandma," I looked down at her with teary eyes. "I don't have anyone else."

"Yes you do, Caleb. You have me, your aunt, and your uncle. We are all your family and we love you very much."

"I know, Gram. But why did they leave? Why right now? They're not even going to see me graduate from high school this year."

Grandma nodded, looking deep into my eyes. "Caleb, I understand how you're feeling right now. You're confused and it's okay to feel that way. Bad things happen to people all the time, but just know that we're going to get through this. Together. You and me. Okay, baby?"

I shook my head, unable to receive her words. "What am I going to do? I have nobody now."

"You have me."

After a few minutes, Dr. Roberts came out again and confirmed that my parents had both died of head injuries and internal bleeding. He told us we could view the bodies, but I didn't want to. My grandmother and aunt chose to go. Once they came back out, they told me that my mom and dad looked okay and they were going to start making funeral arrangements. I barely heard anything they said because I was still in a severe state of shock.

My grandmother touched my arm. "Caleb, your Uncle Cal is going to take you by your house to get some clothes. You're going to stay at my house."

"Okay," I muttered.

I didn't really want to see my parents in the condition they were in after the accident, because that wasn't how I wanted to remember them. However, my curiosity combined with knowing that I would never see them alive again sent me running back toward the viewing area.

I couldn't fight my tears as I sobbed wildly. "I love you! What am I supposed to do without you! What am I supposed to do?" I screamed. That was all I could say. I repeated it over and over.

Uncle Cal walked up behind me and threw an arm around my shoulder. The nurses looked on with pity as they shook their heads at my situation. *I don't need any of your pity. Your stares can't bring either of my parents back!* I thought angrily. After I'd calmed down enough to stand up straight, my Uncle Cal led me out of the room for what seemed like the longest walk of my life. Everyone was looking at me. My grandmother gave me another hug, telling me she loved me.

I couldn't even will myself to say, "I love you, too." The lump growing in the back of my throat kept me from speaking any more words.

I felt like my whole world had ended. I was still in a state of shock and could not believe that my parents were gone. I was all alone.

Feeling empty and sad, I asked my uncle Cal to take me over Mark's house, so I could talk to him. He told me that I should get some rest, but I didn't agree. However, I didn't have the strength to argue with him. We stopped at Chipotle and I messed over my burrito, picking it apart with my fork. I just couldn't make myself eat. My stomach was turning back and forth, and my mind was everywhere. After about ten minutes of sitting there, listening to the hustle and bustle around us, Uncle Cal suggested that I get the food to go.

When we pulled up to my house, I got out of Uncle Cal's car, staring in awe. About fifteen of our neighbors were in our yard, lighting candles and arranging flowers.

My neighbor, Mr. Radcliff, walked up and gave me a hug. He looked me in my eyes and said, "Caleb, I am sorry for your loss. Just keep your head up. And if you need anything, anything at all, please let me know. We will all be here for you."

I nodded, my eyes looked toward the ground. "Thanks, Mr. Radcliff. If I need you I will give you a call."

After receiving hugs from a dozen or so neighbors, I slid my key into the lock and went inside the house. I could still smell the syrup from the pancakes Mom cooked for Dad that morning. It seemed strange that my mom and dad were not there. It was about six in the evening and, whenever I would get home at that time, they were usually watching the news or waiting for me so we could eat dinner. It dawned on me that my parents were never coming back to our home. This building was no longer a home to the three of us, it was just a house. I would never be able to look at it the same again.

Darkness settled over me as I rummaged through my belongings to find some clothes and a few extra pairs of shoes. I was so deep in thought, I jumped when the house phone rang. I fished the cordless phone out from beneath my comforter and answered it.

"Hello, may I speak to Caleb?"

"Speaking."

"This is Mr. Romanovich, your father's boss."

"Hello, sir," I mumbled.

"I am very sorry for your loss, son. I knew something was wrong when Dave didn't show up at the office this morning. He was always a very punctual man. The police station contacted us this morning after someone saw a clip of the accident scene on the news. If you need anything, please let me know."

Wow, it made the news? I thought. "I will, sir."

"Do you know where we should send the flowers from the office?"

"Not yet, my grandmother is going to start making the funeral arrangements tomorrow morning. Her name is Lois. You can call her, and she'll keep you updated." I gave him the number.

"Okay, thanks, Caleb."

"Goodbye, Mr. Romanovich."

"Bye, Caleb. Be good, now."

"Who was that?" Uncle Cal asked, leaning against my bedroom door frame.

"Dad's boss. He wanted to offer his condolences and to be updated on the funeral arrangements."

"Oh. Do you have everything?

I glanced around my room and nodded.

"Let's make sure everything is locked up."

"Okay."

"Give me a hug, nephew. I know you're hurting. I'm hurting too. That was your mother, but she was also my little sister and I'm going to miss her dearly. We'll get through this together."

As I closed the door to lock up, I began to think of all the great memories I'd had with my parents there and how much I was going to miss the significant roles they had each played in my life. I still could not believe that they were both gone. They were too young to die. Each of them was only in their early forties! I felt anger building up and my blood began to warm my skin. I wondered why God would let something so catastrophic occur. Both of my parents were good people. They each worked hard, went to church, and never hesitated to help anyone in need.

I shook my head so hard, it made my temples throb. "They didn't deserve to die like this, Uncle Cal."

"I know, neph. It hurts." He threw an arm over my shoulder as we walked down the driveway to the car.

Chapter Three

We pulled up to Grandma Lois's house around 6:45, and there were five cars in the driveway. Inside, my cousin Joe and his wife, Laina, were sitting in the family room, talking to Grandma. Aunt Shirley, Uncle Derek, and Aunt Barb were in the kitchen, warming up the food they brought over. They all looked at me and each took turns giving me hugs.

"Are you hungry, Caleb?" My grandmother stood and asked me. Worry lines were etched across her pretty face.

"No, Gram. Uncle Cal took me by Chipotle and I couldn't eat." I held up the bag.

"Son, of course you couldn't eat that mess. Get you something nourishing for your soul and get some rest. Your parents are in God's hands."

"Okay," I said reluctantly, heading to the kitchen.

I took my plate upstairs to the guest bedroom and turned on the TV as I sat down on the bed. I took a small bite of the honey-baked ham and instantly knew it was a mistake. I tried to wash it down with a couple swigs of juice, hoping it would stay down. I felt my stomach lurch a few times and my body grew hot. I grabbed a magazine to fan myself with and moved toward the trashcan.

After a few minutes, the nausea left. I got up and set the plate on the desk across the room. I sighed as I lay across my bed. *I knew it was too soon to think about eating something. My stomach feels crazy right now. I wish everyone would just give me a minute to chill,* I thought, staring up at the ceiling. *I still need to process this, and I haven't had a second alone since I found out.*

I plugged my cell phone into the charger I'd brought from my house. The battery had gone dead and as soon as it got some juice. It started vibrating like crazy. I looked down at the screen. There were seventeen voicemail messages, thirty-one texts, and twenty-eight missed calls on my log. Most of the text read, *Ay Caleb. Heard about your folks. Hit me when you get a chance.*

That put an easy smile on my face.

My friends were really looking out for me. I wasn't ready to respond to anyone at that moment. So, I jumped on Instagram and began scrolling through my feed. A video of a cute little toddler doing the floss dance caught my attention. His little arms and hips were moving so fast. I cracked up for the first time all day. Holding onto that thought while lying on top of the bed helped me finally stop my mind for a second so I could get a decent night's rest.

Over the next few days, more and more people visited my grandmother's house. My aunts, uncles, cousins, friends of the family, and other loved ones stopped by to give their condolences and share stories about my parents. We shared some hilarious memories and reflected on the lives they led. It all helped in temporarily easing some pain.

There were many people whom I didn't know that took the time to tell me about how my folks had helped others, gave to the poor, and taken on leadership volunteer positions with local charities.

Hoping one day I would be able to do things like that, I stopped in my grandmother's room to speak to her. "Hey Gram, I was just thinking, Mom and Dad accomplished a lot in their lives. They seized a lifetime of opportunities and things worked out well for them because they loved the Lord and they loved each other."

"You're right, son. Your mother was so kind and loving. She had a pure heart and her smile was just as beautiful. And your father was a man of God, compassionate with a sense of humor. He made us laugh all the time."

I smiled. "Yeah, Grandma. I guess that's where I got my sense of humor from."

"You're right, Caleb. I miss that comical side of you. But you're grieving right now, so it will come out sooner or later." She chuckled. "Oh, and another thing. You got your good looks from me."

I laughed as she winked. "I know. Everybody always says we look alike."

"Yes, we do. But you also look like your father. He was a very handsome man."

"Thanks, Gram."

"You're welcome, baby. Listen, your aunt and I made the funeral arrangements. It's going to be a double ceremony held on Thursday. The wake will be at noon and the funeral service will be at 1:30 p.m. at my church, The Word Church."

"Okay."

"Caleb, does your father have any family we should reach out to in Cleveland?"

"Nope. He has a second cousin in Dayton, but he is about eighty years old."

"Do you have any way to contact him and let him know what's going on?"

"Yeah, but he might be too old to make it up to Cleveland. I'll call him tonight with the funeral arrangements, though."

"You may want to wait until the morning. I know you've had a long day and you're tired. Get some rest and we will finish getting things together tomorrow."

"Okay, Gram. Goodnight."

"Goodnight, Caleb. Oh, and have you heard from any of your friends from school?"

I smiled. "Yes, some of them have called, but I'm going to take some time to myself before talking to them. No one really understands like family does. Love you."

"Okay, sweetie. You're absolutely right. Love you too."

I closed her bedroom door and jumped on my PlayStation 4 for a little bit before heading to bed. Nothing took my mind off things quite like blowing stuff up.

While lying in bed the next morning, I could smell Grandma cooking her infamous breakfast. The teapot whistled, and I could smell her homemade fluffy biscuits baking in the oven.

I stretched, yawned, and headed into the bathroom to brush my teeth and wash my face. Shortly after, I headed down to the kitchen with a smile on my face.

"Good morning, Gram," I said, rubbing my hands together and looking around the kitchen for the food.

She planted a kiss on my cheek. "Good morning, Caleb. Did you sleep well, son?"

"I did."

She pulled the biscuits out of the oven. "How are you feeling this morning?"

"I actually feel pretty good, Gram. I had some trouble getting to sleep at first, but I remembered what you told me. God is always with me, so eventually, I drifted off to sleep."

"Yes, son. Isaiah twenty-six and three says He is with you and He will keep you in perfect peace."

"Thanks, for your encouraging words. How are *you* feeling?"

"Grandma isn't doing too badly for an eighty-something year-ol' gal." I chuckled as she shook her hips to an imaginary song. Probably a gospel one. "Your laughter is music to my ears! Remember Caleb, we need to encourage each other. Although I've worked hard to be strong for you, I'm hurting too. This is a devastating situation we're dealing with. I could never have imagined one of my own children would pass away before me. That's why we need to lift each other up. Proverbs twenty-seven and seventeen says that iron sharpens iron."

"You're right, Grandma. We'll definitely be there for each other."

"Aww, you're such a wonderful grandson. Come and give me a hug."

As we hugged, someone rang the doorbell.

"Who is it?" Grandma called out.

"It's Ms. Johnson, Caleb's principal." A voice came from outside.

Grandma went to the front door and opened it. "How ya doin, Ms. Johnson? I'm Caleb's grandmother, Ms. Lois."

"Nice to meet you, Ms. Lois. I wanted to check in on you and your family. I know a tragic loss like this must have been very hard on Caleb. The students and faculty want to show our deepest sympathy to you and yours."

"How kind of you. Please step in out of the cold," my grandmother ushered Ms. Johnson into the house.

Once she stomped the snow off her boots, Ms. Johnson turned and looked at me. "Good morning, Caleb."

I walked over and shook her hand. "Good morning, Ms. Johnson. Thanks for stopping by." "No problem. We have a card and flowers for you. Also, if you need to talk to a grief counselor we can set it up for you."

"I'm fine for right now, Ms. Johnson. But thank you for the card and flowers."

"My pleasure. If you need anything, be sure to call the school and we will get you the help you need."

"Thanks."

"I won't hold you guys up from enjoying your breakfast. Nice meeting you, Grandma Lois."

"Same to you, honey. Be blessed, have a good day, and thank you for being so concerned about my Caleb."

"You are very welcome, Ms. Lois. Goodbye, Caleb."

I waved. "Thanks again."

"Bye-bye, honey," my grandmother said, closing the door behind her. "She sure is a nice lady."

"Yeah," I sat, sniffing the flowers absentmindedly.

"Your classmates really care about you."

I nodded while spreading butter on my biscuit before dousing it with honey. I finally had my appetite back and I wasn't going to let it go to waste. "Yeah. They could have sent them to the church, but her bringing them here really lifted my spirits."

Grandma reached up to pinch my cheek before setting the flowers in a vase. "There's that handsome smile I've been missing!"

Friends and family continued to stop by the house to express their condolences and share memories of my parents throughout the day and the next evening.

"Caleb...Caleb!" I heard my grandma call out.

I was downstairs playing a video game. *She is always calling me,* I thought. "Yes, Gram?"

"Your cell phone is ringing."

I went upstairs and saw that I had a missed call from Mark. I called him right back.

"Hey, what's up, C," He answered.

"Hey, Mark. What's good?"

"I just called to see how you were doing. I haven't heard from you and wanted to give you a little time before I hit you back."

"Yeah, everything's everything. Just been taking some time out with the family. Laying low, getting ready for tomorrow."

"I know, man. As the only child, you probably feel like you're all alone now. But we're homies and I'm here. Why don't you let me pick you up for a quick ride? Maybe you need to get out of the house for a minute."

"Good idea."

"Okay. On my way in five."

I went downstairs to tell grandma I was going to hang out with Mark. She said, "Okay, but be back by eleven. You know we've got to get up early and get ready for the funeral."

"Yeah."

Just before I walked out the door, I heard my grandmother say, "Caleb, is your suit ready?"

"Yeah. The cleaners called earlier and said I'm good to pick it up at seven."

"Okay. Be safe. I love you," she shouted as I closed the door.

"Okay, I will. Love you too."

"I want some ice cream bad," I said.

Mark me drove over to Dairy Queen. "Ice cream? You normally drink slushies," Mark said, with a raised eyebrow.

"Oh, so I have to be confined to just drinking slushies because you said so?"

Mark looked at me for a second before saying, "Man, watch your tone. It was a simple comment."

I immediately felt guilty for snapping at him. "Ay man, my bad. I didn't mean to snap you up."

Mark shrugged his shoulders. "You're good, man, I know you're going through it right now."

While we were ordering our food, I saw Yvonne walk in with her parents, who immediately walked over, offering their condolences. I thanked them.

"Hey. How are you, Caleb?" Yvonne's voice was laced with sympathy, but I could tell she was happy to see me.

"Hey, Yvonne."

"I heard about your mom and dad. I tried texting you, but you left me on read."

I nodded. "Yeah, my bad. Thanks for reaching out. I just haven't really been up to responding to anyone yet."

She smiled. "I totally understand. I mean... I guess I can't possibly understand... but..."

I shook my head. "Don't worry about it. You're good."

She blushed. "Well, do you mind if I come to the funeral tomorrow?"

"Not at all," I smiled at her, glad that she asked. "It's at The Word Church. The wake starts at noon and the funeral is at one-thirty." Then I thought about something. "Your parents are cool with you missing school tomorrow?"

She nodded. "Ms. Johnson said if any of the students and teachers wanted to show their support, we could have an early release day." She paused. "Here," she said, handing me a napkin she'd written her number down on. "Be sure to lock me in and call me anytime you need me.

Maybe we can hang out at the movies or go bowling with some friends."

"Okay. I'll see you tomorrow. Thanks."

"No problem. Bye, Caleb." She gave me that finger wave I love.

Chapter Four

It was 3:30 p.m. on a chilly, rainy Thursday afternoon. I felt completely numb as I stood at the Grace Mount Cemetery in the heart of Cleveland, laying my mom and dad to rest. As my grandmother's pastor read a collection of passages from the Bible, all I could think about was saying my final goodbyes to my parents. It was at that moment that I realized I was really on my own. At 17, could I handle the pressure of having no parents? I still felt like I had so much to learn. Who was going to be there to teach me everything I needed to know?

When the pastor said, "Ashes to ashes, dust to dust," there was an outburst of people crying and moaning. Grandma squeezed my hand and I squeezed hers back. We walked over to the caskets, picked up some of the flowers, knelt, and blew kisses to them both.

I said, "Mom and Dad, I will always love and remember you. I'll see you both again someday."

Once we got back to Grandma's house, we had a homegoing party like no other. All my family and friends came and there were various types of foods. My Aunt Shirley even made my favorite dessert, strawberry-marbled cheesecake.

With the funeral behind me, my appetite had finally fully returned, and I was ready to smash. We had a good time laughing, dancing, singing, and occasionally crying. However, when people started to leave, reality threatened my brief sense of comfort again.

I felt kind of tired, so I laid down for a moment, thanking God the funeral was finally over and wondering about my future. That's when Grandma called me.

"Caleb... Caleb?

"Yeah?" I answered.

"Are you sleeping?" she asked.

"No, I'm lying down for a minute."

"Can you come here and help me with the dishes?"

Her request stunned me, and I went downstairs to answer her question. "Grandma, I don't wash dishes. My mom would always do them. The only thing I did was take out the garbage and yardwork."

"That's good, son, but I'm going to show you how to take out the trash *and* wash the dishes, so you'll be well-rounded in the future. When you have your own place in the near future, those dishes aren't going to wash themselves."

"Okay, Grandma," I said, respectfully trying to hide my annoyance. It had been a long day and I just wanted to chill alone with my thoughts.

"How do you feel?" she asked, handing me a towel.

"I feel fine, Gram," I said, studying her hands in the soapy water.

She kept her eyes on me. "Are you glad it's all over now?"

"Yes, I am. It was a very tiresome day and now I have to make sure things are in place. Being the only child is rough. I wish I had an older brother or sister to help me with things. I'm only seventeen and I can't imagine having to be responsible for myself," I said, venting about some of the concerns that had been building all week.

"One day soon, you will be grown, son," Grandma said.

"But there's one decision I have made for myself."

"What's that Caleb?"

"I would like to live with you, Grandma," I told her. "Will you be my guardian for the next few months?"

"That's great! Of course, I will, son. This house is your home. We're family," she said, smiling and drying her hands so she could place one on my shoulder. "There is one thing, though."

"What's that, Gram?" I asked.

"You've got to live by my rules."

I groaned inwardly. "What are the rules?"

Gesturing with her right hand, she numbered the rules for me. "Number one, respect me at all times. Number two, do not bring any females to the house when I am not at home. Number three, make sure all your homework is finished before you go out with your friends. And, number four, make sure your chores are done. That means your bedroom is clean and the kitchen is clean before you go to bed. That includes the dishes, stove, table, floor, and trash. Deal?"

I had completely zoned out while Grandma went on her rant. When I heard she'd finally stopped talking and asked me something, I nodded and echoed the last word. "Deal."

"Oh, and another thing. Sweep down the steps once a month."

"Yes, Gram."

"And one more thing..."

Don't you mean 'fifth more thing'?

"...on school nights, your curfew is nine. On weekends, it's eleven. You'll need to check in at ten-thirty and let me know you're on your way home."

"Wait, Gram. My folks let me stay out 'til midnight on weekends."

"Caleb, I'm looking out for your best interest. I just want to keep you out of harm's way and trouble, son."

Judging from the expression on her face, I knew there was no use in trying to debate about it.

"Got it, Gram."

After watching ESPN's late-night edition, I started to get sleepy. I walked past my grandmother's bedroom on my way to my own. It sounded like she was having a conversation with someone. I assumed she was on the phone with one of her church friends.

Then I heard her say, "Bless, Caleb. Please give him a future and hope, as you promise in Jeremiah twenty-nine and eleven. Keep him from evil. Surround him with your loving angels. He is the head and not the tail. He is above and not beneath, as Deuteronomy twenty-eight and thirteen states. He is the lender and not the borrower. And as you tell us in Isaiah fifty-four and seventeen, no weapon formed against him shall prosper. Comfort him with the love of Christ. I ask all this in Jesus's name, Amen."

I listened in, moved by her love for me and her faith in God. I continued to my room and knelt on the floor, asking God to watch over her and thanking Him for giving me such a wonderful grandmother, a grandmother who prayed for me.

Early the next morning, while cleaning my room, Grandma knocked on the door.

"Good morning, Caleb."

"Morning, Gram."

"Do you want some oatmeal?"

I nodded. "You know that's my favorite."

"Butter and brown sugar?"

"Yeah. Can you add a little condensed milk too?"

"You got it, son. I made you two pieces of toast and there's a glass of orange juice on the counter."

As we sat down to eat, she said, "Son, I am so glad to have you here, despite the circumstances."

"I like it here too, Gram, but I really miss home," I said.

"I know you do, but trust and believe, things will work out for your good. What are your plans and dreams? After all, you are a senior in high school. Are you still thinking about going to Ohio State University?"

"Yes. I applied at the beginning of the school year and was accepted. But since everything has happened, I don't know about the financial part of it. I have a few scholarships, but they won't cover tuition, books, and room and board."

"Well, congratulations! I want you to know that you are the sole beneficiary of your parents' estate and they set up a trust fund when you were eight years old."

I lifted an eyebrow. "Really? How much is it worth?"

"It's worth eighty thousand dollars."

"Eighty thousand?"

"Yes, son. You can go to OSU," she smiled warmly.

I looked up at the ceiling, silently thanked my parents and God, and gave my grandmother a big hug.

"Caleb, your parents were very good to you and they had been planning for your future ever since you were born. They were always very frugal, but they put their money where it mattered most, in your future."

"Apparently. That's why I want to go to college and make something of myself, so their sacrifice will mean something."

Grandma gazed at me and smiled. "Son, you're a lot like me when I was your age. All I wanted to do was make my parents proud of me. Even though they couldn't afford to send me off to college, I was determined to make the best of things. I cleaned houses, babysat, and worked as a porter at a hotel. Nothing was given to me and I had to work hard all my life."

"Gram, tell me about your childhood."

"It was tough, but we made it."

"Can you tell me about your parents?"

"Yes, yes, yes. I had the most wonderful father and mother. They were very loving, but also very stern, which was needed. My father had the most impact on me because some of the things he thought and shared with me, I still use today. Don't get me wrong, my mother taught me how to cook and be a lady, but my dad was the go-getter.

He did whatever he needed to do for his family to survive."

I nodded, fully engaged and interested. I had never taken the time to talk with her beyond surface topics and was intrigued by her story. "Gram, how old were you when you got married?"

"I was nineteen and your grandpa was twenty-one. He was in the navy and I was a freshman in college. It was nineteen forty-six and the second war was over. I got pregnant with your mother and then your grandpa came to visit his brother in Cleveland. He got your grandfather a job at the Chevy plant where he worked for nearly thirty-five years. After he retired, he made me miserable with hurtful words and abusive behavior all day long. After thirty years of marriage, I couldn't take it any longer. I left him and got my own apartment, which was hard because it was my first time living on my own. I'd basically went from under my father's roof to under my husband's roof. He would visit me from time to time, but he would never say he wanted me back."

She went on. "So, one day, I got a call at work from one of the neighbors saying that my husband had a stroke and the mailman had seen him slumped over on the floor in the living room."

"For the next three months, he was confined to a hospital bed in the ICU on a breathing machine. I went back home and prayed for that man. I told God, even though he didn't treat me right, I still wanted Him to bless him and I prayed for his salvation. And you know what, Caleb? Since he's been gone, I have peace in my heart because God knows that I did my best to be a good wife and mother."

A few moments of thoughtful silence passed before I spoke. "Whoa, Gram. I never knew any of those details."

"Yeah, well, you're almost grown now, so it was time you knew. Sometimes your test becomes your testimony."

"I've always heard you say that. What exactly does that mean?"

"It means God allows things to happen in your life to test your character and to see if you can endure the bad times. God will always be near you. Just trust Him, no matter how long He takes. Psalm fifty-six and three tells us He will turn things around in your life for you, if you just believe."

"I do believe in a higher power, Gram. But I can't see Him. I want to know God for myself, but it seems kind of strange talking to someone who doesn't say anything back to you."

"I understand just what you're talking about. Hebrews eleven and one tells us it takes faith to know He is real. But, take a look at the leaves outside. They were once green in August, various colors in October and they're all gone now. Something you can see was changed by something you can't see. But you have faith that they will all return in a couple of months. Son, always remember what second Corinthians five and seven says: that we walk by faith and not by sight. Don't believe what you see because this whole world is passing away. But believe in what you cannot see."

"Gram, you spit those hot Bible bars for days. We need to get you in the studio," I chuckled.

"Start studying the Bible faithfully like I do, and you'll be lit for Christ, too. You'll also get most of your life questions answered." She elbowed me and winked. We both cracked up as we began clearing the table.

Later that evening, I could smell a delicious aroma filling the house. "Mmm-mmm, what are you making, Gram?"

"A lemon pound cake."

"Can I get at that mixing bowl and those beaters when you're done?"

"Yeah. You remind me of your mother. She used to enjoy running her finger around the bowl, eating the leftover cake mix."

I flinched at my grandmother's choice of words. It was hard to hear "used to" and my mother in the same sentence.

I wanted to drown my sorrows in food. "Oh, and can I have the icing bowl, too?"

"Sure. I'm glad you have your appetite back, son. Now, can you do me a favor?"

"Yeah."

"Please clean these few dishes for me," she said, more as a directive than a request.

"Uh... no, Grandma. Remember, I don't do dishes. That's for women."

"What did you just say, Caleb?"

"I'm used to the roles that were represented in my home. My mom cleaned the house and my dad worked to take care of the family."

Grandma wiped her hands on a dish towel, as she turned to look at me. "Yes, honey, that's true, about your former household. But remember, sometimes the wife may need a break from cooking and cleaning. That's when the man steps in to take the pressure off her because he loves and cares for her and is willing to help in any way possible."

"Yeah, I guess you're right, Gram."

"Son, whenever you can, always be eager to help someone else, because you just don't know when that someone in need might be you."

"Gram, I understand what you're saying, but sometimes it can be a bit much. It feels like you're always trying to force God on me. Mom and Dad believed in God, but they let me figure things out for myself."

"Caleb! I am not trying to force my God on you. The same God that loves me loves you. Jesus Christ, His only son, died for me and you."

"I know, Grandma, but I'm still angry at Him right now. If He is the so-called Savior, why couldn't He save my folks?"

The anger and resentment I'd felt since the accident rose to the surface. I hadn't taken the time to articulate it and it felt like my insides were imploding.

My grandmother's eyes softened, and she gazed at me for a moment before speaking. "Caleb, saving your mom and dad in the accident was not in His will. Giving them eternal life was."

Chapter Five

On Saturday, at about one o'clock in the afternoon, my grandmother and I were grocery shopping and running a few errands when I got a call from Mark.

After our usual small talk, he asked, "What are you going to be doing around three thirty?"

I shrugged. "Nothing."

"Roll to the mall with us."

"All right. You picking me up?"

"No, we're going to catch the bus on Liberty Avenue."

"Okay, who else is coming?" I asked putting a case of water of bottled water in my grandmother's cart for her.

"George and Pete. We'll meet you at the bus stop at three thirty."

"Okay, text me when you leave the house."

"All right, later," Mark said.

"Who was that, son?" Grandma asked.

"Mark. Is it cool if I go to the mall with him and a couple of my friends?"

"Sure, Caleb, I don't mind. You need to get out with friends. You've been stuck in the house ever since you came to live with me. Get out and enjoy yourself. But remember to call at ten-thirty and be home by eleven."

I nodded. "Bet. Thanks, Gram."

After we got home, I finished doing a few chores around the house, then called Mark.

"I was just about to call you. My sister is going to let me use her car for the rest of the day, so I'll pick you up in about ten minutes. Text me the address."

"Okay."

While Grandma was relaxing in her recliner and watching TV, I walked up and said, "Hey, Gram. I'm leaving out."

She bent over and reached in her purse. "Okay. Be careful and always be aware of your surroundings. Call me if you need me and stay away from trouble." She handed me a couple twenty-dollar bills.

I thanked her and gave her a kiss on the cheek before walking out to the front porch.

I heard Mark approaching before I saw him. I quickly looked around to see if anyone else was outside. It was a predominately older neighborhood. His sounds were booming heavily as he bumped Future's latest single. I walked over to the left rear car door and got in.

"What's up, C?"

"What's good, Mark? Hey, George. What's up, Pete?"

"Nothing, C. Just ready to grab some new J's," George said.

"I'm sorry to hear about what happened to your folks, bro. How've you been holding up?" Pete asked.

"Thanks, man. Just maintaining," I muttered, not wanting to discuss it further.

"Is this where you're living now?" George asked.

"Yeah. With my mom's mom," I said, scrolling through my Instagram feed.

"That's what's up. When are you coming back to school?" Pete asked.

"Hopefully Monday," I said, stopping to look at a selfie Yvonne posted. I looked at a few of the comments, then liked it. "My grandmother's cool, but she got so many rules and I'm not used to all that. Gotta meet with Ms. Johnson and the school's grief counselor and then... I never thought I'd say this... I'll be so pumped to get back in school."

"Grandma, I'm ghost!" Pete yelled.

We all laughed, grateful for the lightened mood. George shook his head. "I know you can't wait for that, man. You'll be coming back just in time for prom. Y'all going?"

"Yeah," Mark said, "...if I can find a date."

George and Pete said they were going without dates. George added, "Man, I don't need no date. I'm going to know everyone up in there, so I'll just fly dolo."

"Maybe we can split a limo between the four of us," Pete suggested. "Mark?"

"I'll think about it," Mark said, his eyes on the road.

I was still undecided. I wanted to go to prom, but I didn't want to go with a bunch of guys. I honestly wanted Yvonne on my arm. "I'll let you guys know for sure by next week."

We arrived at the mall and the first stop was Macy's.

"Ay, let's go to the fragrance counter for some free samples," Mark suggested.

"Oh yeah! I gotta stay fresh for the ladies."

"Right, granny and mama like they're boy smelling sweet," Pete cracked. We all cracked up.

My phone rang, and I answered it.

"Hey, Caleb."

"Hey, Von. What are you up to?"

"I'm fine, just thinking about you. I didn't want to text you. Guess I wanted to hear your voice instead. What have you been up to?"

I smiled. "Pretty much chillin'. Just ready to get back to school."

I heard an exaggerated gasp on the other end. "Did I call Caleb's phone?"

I chuckled. "So, you're a comedian, now?

"Maybe. So, what are you up to today?"

"At the mall with a few friends."

"That's funny. A few of my girls and I are headed that way. Wanna meet at the food court at three forty-five?"

"That'll work. See you there."

After we hung up, I headed over to grab a Gucci sample from the cologne counter. "Hey, fellas. Yvonne is headed up here with her girls. She's going to meet us at the food court in fifteen."

Mark said, "I hope her girls are fine like her."

"Ay man, kill that. You don't need to concern yourself about how she looks," I warned him.

Mark just smirked before changing the subject. "Hey, let's go to GameStop right quick. I need to trade in a couple games for that NBA 2K nineteen."

We walked over to the store and browsed around for a bit before we were greeted by the clerk. Mark informed the clerk that he wanted to trade in his games. He looked about our age and seemed to be the only one in the store.

"All right, man. What games do you have?"

"These." Mark slid the games across the counter.

"And which game did you want?"

"NBA 2K nineteen."

"That's cool." The clerk took a closer look at Mark. "Hey, you look kind of familiar. I'm Jim."

"What's up, man? I'm Michael."

I lifted an eyebrow thoughtfully but remained silent.

"That's cool. Well, we have NBA 2K nineteen right here, but your two trades will only get you about thirty-five dollars. NBA 2K nineteen is sixty-five dollars. Would you like to pay the difference in credit card or cash?"

"Cash. May I see it first?"

Jim walked over to unlock the case, then handed Mark the game. The store phone rang. Jim locked the case and walked back over to the desk. "Excuse me for a moment, guys. Hello? Yes... okay. It says we have it in stock, but I haven't seen that one on the shelf. I'll have to double check in the back for you." He placed the call on hold before turning to us and said, "One second, fellas. I need to check on something for a customer. Wait here for a second."

As soon Jim walked to the back room, George immediately said, "Rookie mistake. Let's go."

"What, you don't want the game, Mark?" I asked, confused.

"No, fool! Grab *all* the games and let's roll!" George snapped.

I hesitated for a second. Then I put the new game in my coat while Mark grabbed his other two games. We walked out as quickly as we could, and extreme guilt got the best of me. As we walked toward the elevator, I saw Pete on his phone and realized he never went inside the store with us.

"Did you get it?" he asked as we got on the elevators.

We heard the man shouting as the doors closed. "Hey! Stop those guys, they're stealing. Security! Security!"

"Where were you, Pete?" I asked, my heart racing.

He looked cool as a cucumber as he smirked at me. "Who do you think the caller was?"

"Why did we get on this slow elevator? We should have taken the escalator!" George groaned.

"When these doors open, we have to go our separate ways. Let's meet at my car in twenty minutes," Mark instructed.

"Bet," I said, rubbing my sweaty palms on my joggers.

Once the elevator doors opened, we scattered, walking briskly toward the various exits. Mark, Pete, and George had all chosen the right directions. I walked past the coffee shop and turned right at the bath and body store. I saw an exit sign lit up in the distance. I headed in that direction, planning to take the stairwell that would lead outside. I looked around to see if anyone was on my tail and it seemed like I was home free to make it the five hundred feet to the door, I would hide out in the parking lot, ducking between the cars until it was time to head over to meet the others.

I pulled out my phone to text Yvonne that I would have to meet her later. Just as I reached the door, I felt a heavy hand land on my shoulder. I closed my eyes for a second before turning around to face whoever had caught up with me, wishing it was one of my friends, but knowing it likely was not. I opened them to find myself face to face with a stern-faced mall security guard. I hung my head in surrender.

"Got one," he spoke into his radio. Then he ordered, "Open your jacket. Now!"

I slowly opened my jacket and the video game clattered to the floor.

He stooped down to retrieve it. "Do you have a receipt for this?"

I shook my head, which was still hanging in shame.

He grabbed my arm and pulled me back toward the center of the mall. "Well, it looks like your friends ditched you and you're the one left holding the bag. Come with me."

We took the walk of shame that I'd seen so many other young adults take in the past. Never did I ever think I would be taking that same path. I kept my eyes on the floor until something told me to look up. Just as I did, saw Yvonne and three of her friends I recognized from school standing and watching in shock.

"Caleb, what happened?" she called out.

I didn't know what to say as the guard handed me over to a police officer, who led me away. I finally found the words to call out over my shoulder, "Von, do me a favor. Please call my grandmother and tell her to come and get me from the police station, okay?"

Everyone stared at me while the officer led me out to the parking lot to put me in a waiting patrol car. I was humiliated. A couple of my schoolmates had their phones out, recording me, and some of their parents were there, watching and shaking their heads.

Chapter Six

When we got to the police station, I had to fill out some paperwork and was able to make one phone call. I didn't want to call my grandmother because I knew she was probably on her way and was already very upset with me. I chose to call Uncle Cal on his cell phone.

"Hello, Uncle Cal? This is Caleb."

"Hi, Caleb." I could hear the disappointment in his voice. I didn't have to ask him if he knew.

"We're on our way to get you."

"Okay. Can I speak to Grandma?"

"Yeah, she's right here."

"Hey Gram," I stammered.

"Don't 'Gram' me. Boy, you've got a lot of

explaining to do!"

"I know, Grandma. I don't know what I was thinking. Before I knew it, I'd made a terrible mistake. I know you're disappointed."

"Disappointed is an understatement! Have I not told you to stay out of trouble and to be aware of your surroundings? And I heard you were stealing. Listen, I don't want to even talk to you right now, let alone see you. I'll see you once we get to the station. Goodbye." She hung up on me.

I trudged back to the holding cell, with my head down and feeling depressed. An officer said to me, "This is your first offense, so your bond is set at five thousand dollars."

I panicked. "What? Five stacks? My grandmother doesn't have that kind of money on hand."

"No, young man. Your folks don't need to come up with the whole thing. They only need to come up with ten percent, which is five hundred dollars. Once you arrive at your court date, they'll get it back."

"Thank God," I said with a sigh of relief.

"But you still may end up doing community service. I sure hope you've learned your lesson. I hate to see young men like you within these walls," the officer said.

"I will, sir. You're never going to see me in here again, officer. This place is not for me."

"I hear you. You seem to have good sense, but you've got to make the right choices. What's your name?"

"Caleb, Officer..."

"Ben Brown."

"Nice to meet you, Officer Brown. Thanks for the words of wisdom."

I had about twenty more minutes after Mr. Brown left to be alone with my thoughts. *I can't even believe this! I waited until I became a seventeen-year-old orphan to land myself in jail doing this dumb stuff. It wasn't even my stupid game, but I allowed myself to be talked into this. And where are the people who talked me into it? Who knows!*

About ten minutes later, Officer Brown returned to my cell and said, "Caleb, your family is here to pick you up."

As he opened the door to let me out, I felt like a liberated slave who had just been emancipated.

Grandma and Uncle Cal were waiting for me in the lobby when I was finally released. I tried to hug grandma, but she turned slightly. In a soft tone, she said, "Caleb I am very disappointed in you. First of all, you didn't need to steal anything. All you needed to do was ask for what you wanted, and I would have tried to help you get it. Secondly, I've told you since you were a child, to stay out of trouble. Boy, you'd better be careful who you hang around with. You know birds of a feather flock together."

"Not all the time, Grandma. I have good friends. It was me who decided to steal. Nobody forced me into it. I did it because I wanted to see if I would get caught."

"Caleb, just how foolish are you?"

"I made a mistake and I don't want to make the same one again. I know you're disappointed in me and forgiving me will take some time."

"Son, I've already forgiven you, but you are on punishment. You can't go anywhere but school for two weeks. No friends over and you can only use the computer for schoolwork. Also, when we get home, give me your PlayStation and phone."

"My games? I'm going to be bored to death in that house without them!"

"Then read a book," she said as we walked to the car.

"Books put me to sleep."

"Boy, I don't want to hear all that back talk! Just do what I tell you."

Knowing better than pushing her any further, I sulked silently after replying, "Yes, Grandma."

Mark text me as soon as I walked in the door. I couldn't believe he had the nerve to hit my phone up after the stunt he pulled.

I rolled my eyes. *Glad this dude thinks this is all a joke. Meanwhile, I due in court next week for his mess. Typical Mark.*

So I gotta chill out for a minute until things boil over

Ok C. I agree, you shouldn't rock the boat. But, if u change ur mind and decide to go, u can ride with me

Alright. Later.

After a few yawns, I put my cell phone on the charger and laid down. I thought about why I'd stolen the game. Part of me didn't know why, but another part of me did. I really enjoyed the adrenaline rush that came from doing it. It was

almost like I stepped outside of myself and was watching it all happen. Quite honestly, after the trauma of losing my parents and being cooped up under my grandmother, it felt good to stop thinking about my problems and doing something so exciting. I felt like a seventeen-year-old again. On the other hand, the consequences canceled it all out. In hindsight, it just wasn't worth it at all.

I drifted off to sleep and began to dream. Well actually, I don't know if I was dreaming or not. The only thing I remember is that I started feeling kind of strange. I was trying to get up from the bed, but it felt like someone or something was holding me down. My breath seemed to leave me, getting shorter and shorter by the second and I couldn't move. I felt like I was going to die.

"Somebody please help me! Help me!" I yelled. Then I called on him, "Jesus, Jesus, Jesus, Jesus!"

When I came to, I was drenched in a cold sweat and trembling. I looked up to see my grandmother at my bedside.

"Caleb... Caleb? You all right, son? It looks like you had a bad dream," she said shaking me.

"Yeah. What time is it?" I said while sitting up and wiping the sweat from my face.

"It's about seven-thirty a.m., and I see you slept in your clothes."

"Yeah, I guess I did. I was only going to lie down for a moment. I must have fallen asleep and had a terrible dream. It seemed as if someone was holding me down and every time I tried to get up, my breath would get shorter and shorter. That's when I thought I was going to die. But when I called on Jesus, I immediately woke up."

My grandmother reached out and stroked my head. It was the first time she'd touched me since I had been arrested. "Son, it sounds like God is trying to reach you. You have to heed and listen to His word. He only wants to help you."

I nodded, still rubbing my eyes and trying to shake off the chill of my recent dream.

"Each night, before you go to bed, say your prayers and read the Bible. It will give you comfort and peace. Just believe me when I tell you, the Lord will keep you safe, Caleb."

"All I know is I don't want to feel that helpless ever again!"

"Son, Philippians four and seven tells us to always keep our heart and minds on Christ Jesus. He will protect you. Listen to me Caleb, He will never leave you or forsake you. I am a living witness," she said, rubbing my shoulder and nodding her head matter-of-factly.

"Aw, Gram. I'm listening, but you keep on preaching to me like I'm a hopeless or something. It was only a dream. It's not that serious."

"No, son, I don't think you're hopeless. But with all that I know about Christ Jesus and His unfailing love, it would be devastating if I did not tell you more about Him."

"I understand, and I know you mean well Gram, but I want to come to know Him for myself, in my own time," I told her. I smiled slightly so she wouldn't think I was being disrespectful.

"You will get to know Him, soon and very soon. Get up and get ready for church." I nodded, and she left the room, closing the door behind her. I showered, got dressed, and went downstairs to eat.

I finished my cereal, washed the few dishes in the sink, grabbed my coat, and went out the front door. I just wanted to wait for my Uncle Cal outside and to get some fresh air. I was still reeling from my "near-death" experience. My grandmother came out a few moments later and Uncle Cal arrived just as she locked the door.

We arrived at church promptly at ten a.m. "Gram, do you mind if I sit in the balcony with my friends from school?" I asked her after noticing some friends on the upper level of the sanctuary.

"No, I don't mind," she said as she made her way to her seat.

I saw Yvonne at the top of the stairs and she waved me over.

"Hey, Caleb!" she smiled warmly as I sat down.

"What's up, Yvonne?"

"I didn't know you belonged to this church."

"I don't, actually. My grandmother belongs here. That's why we had my parents' homegoing service here. I'm just visiting."

"Oh, okay. We've been coming here since we moved here. I think you'll like it."

I nodded. "Hey, thanks for calling my grandmother the other day for me," I said, looking down at my hands.

She touched my knee. "No problem."

I would never say anything to Yvonne about it, but I was still very embarrassed about what she saw at the mall the other day. I couldn't believe she was still acting so cool, seeing it all had just happened. *She doesn't even think about judging me. Man, I really like this girl.*

The choir, decked in black and gold robes, rose to their feet and sang two powerful and moving selections. I sat back in the pew, closed my eyes, and enjoyed the music.

The preacher's sermon wasn't as lively as the music and I quickly grew bored. I grabbed a piece of paper and wrote, *Do you like me? Check*

YES or NO. I gave it to Yvonne and she smirked. To my surprise, she put a check mark next to yes. She also wrote, "And you're corny for this" with a smiley face next to it.

After service was over, we talked for a moment. She invited me to Teen Church the next Saturday, but I knew I wanted to go to the party with my friends, so I told her I would let her know later.

During our ride home, my grandmother asked, "Son, did you enjoy the service?"

"Yes, I did. The choir was dope."

"What do you mean by *dope?*" she asked, confused.

"My bad, Gram. It's slang for very good."

"Son, you know I'm an old lady, so you have to break it down for me. I thought y'all young folks still used 'da bomb'."

I'm dead, I thought as I cracked up at my grandmother's attempt to stay current. "Yup, same thing, Gram."

She shook her head and waved her hand in dismissal. "I'm not going to even pretend like I know the new lingo you young folks are using."

Uncle Cal and I laughed.

"I don't know about y'all but I could eat a horse," Grandma said. "And I don't feel like cooking."

"Let's go to that buffet place that has the steak and fried shrimp. What's the name of it, Uncle Cal?"

"Oh, you're talking about The Golden Corral."

"Yes, that's it. What do you think, Grandma?"

She gave a thumbs up and said, "Sounds like a plan."

"Ditto," said Uncle Cal. Fifteen minutes later, we pulled into the parking lot and the place was packed, as usual. The line extended all the way outside the door, but we waited patiently. When we finally were seated, we ate well. My stomach was so full, I was good for the rest of the day.

Later that evening, while I was ironing my clothes for school, I started to think about my mom and dad. Tears streamed down my face non-stop and I didn't even try to stop them. My grief counselor told me to sit with my pain instead of running from it. Since I rarely got time to myself, I decided to follow that advise. A few minutes later, my grandmother knocked on the door, then came into the room without waiting for an answer.

"Son, are you all right?"

"Yes, Gram, but dag, I could have been naked in here!" I said, wiping my face.

"Boy, you don't have anything I haven't seen before. I changed your very first diaper and hundreds after that one!" When she noticed my wet eyes, her jokes ceased. "What's wrong, son?"

"Everything's okay. I was just wondering how different things would be if Mom and Dad were still alive."

"What do you mean?"

"I don't know. It just seems like I don't have anyone to talk to or share a conversation with and how I'm really feeling inside."

"Son, whenever you feel the need to talk, just let me know and I will be there for you. I know you're still mourning the loss of your parents. I am too, Caleb. So, I may need you to encourage me every now and then as well," she said compassionately.

"Gram, you're right. That wasn't just my loss. That was your daughter and son-in-law also.

Thanks for reminding me that I'm not the only one grieving. We should encourage each other more every day."

She smiled. "Son, if you would like to talk to one of the elders at the church, I can make that happen for you."

"Thanks, Gram. I'll let you know."

"Also, talk to God. He's waiting on you to call on Him and anything and everything is found in Him. Try it, you will never go wrong by doing so."

I nodded. "Thanks for your advice. When I'm ready, I will."

"Son, there is no better time than now."

"Well, what should I do, just start randomly talking to Him?"

"Speak to Him just like you speak to me. Tell Him how you're feeling. Don't be afraid Caleb, for God is always with you."

Chapter Seven

I was excited about my first day back to school. It seemed like I had been gone for a long time. I walked up to my locker, which was decorated with welcome back signs and balloons. Every teacher I came in contact with welcomed me back happily. Even students I didn't know went out of their way to greet me. During lunch, a few friends and I were eating when Yvonne stopped by.

"Hi, everyone. Caleb, welcome back."

"Hey, Yvonne, I saw you in third period, but you didn't see me."

She smiled. "Have you given any more thought about going to Teen Church with me on Saturday?"

Dag, I was hoping she wouldn't ask me again. I need an excuse, I thought.

"Yes, I'd love to, but I'll have to ask my grandmother because I'm still grounded. I'm going to lay low for a little while longer before asking her." I said. "I'll text you in a couple of days."

"Okay, don't forget," she said, smiling as she walked away.

I watched her walk away until she was no longer in view before turning around to talk to my friends. I was surprised to find they were all looking at me.

"You know she likes you, C," Mark said.

I shrugged it off. "We're just friends. She wants me to visit her church again on Saturday."

"That's the day of the party."

"I know."

Just then, an idea popped into my head of how I could please everyone, including myself. "I'll go to the party with you after Teen Church.

I'll tell my grandmother I'm going to church, stay there for a quick minute, then go to the party," I said, shoving the rest of my food into my mouth so I wouldn't be late for my next class.

Mark nodded. "Sounds like a plan to me, C."

I went straight home after school. Grandma was gone but she left me a note, reminding me to clean my room and to wash the dishes. Just as I turned on the TV to play my video game, Aunt Shirley and Grandma pulled in the driveway. A few seconds, later, I heard, "Caleb... Caleb! Come to the side door."

Whew! I thought as I turned the TV back off.

Almost got busted.

"Hey, Gram."

"Hey, son. Can you get the groceries out of your Aunt Shirley's car?"

"Yes, ma'am."

I was halfway to the door when she said, "Son, put on your coat. It's cold outside. And put something on your head."

"Hi, Caleb." Aunt Shirley greeted me as I helped her with the rest of the bags.

"Hey, how are you, Auntie Shirley?" "Fine and you?"

"I've been okay. Just trying to finish school. I need a summer job. Can you get me on where you work?"

"Yes, Caleb. They're always hiring. I'll look on the website and call you toward the end of the week. But, I have to run back out to pick up your Uncle Cal. Love you."

"Love you too, Auntie. Bye."

When I went back inside the house, Grandma asked, "How was your day in school?"

"It was fine. Everybody was glad I was back, including my teachers."

"Do you have any homework?"

I shook my head. "No, Gram, I got it all done in study hall."

"That's good. Thank you for washing those dishes."

"No problem."

"Are you hungry, son?"

"No. I made a ham sandwich before you got here."

"Okay. Well, I think I'll make some sloppy joes for dinner. Would you like to have some steak fries to go along with them?"

"Yeah, that sounds good."

"Did anybody call for me?"

"Nope. Hey, Gram."

"Yes?"

"My friend Yvonne invited me to Teen Church on Saturday. Is it cool if I go?"

"You can go but have Yvonne's parents call me first."

"Okay."

All week long, I was filled with anticipation. I wanted so badly for things to go smoothly so I could get out of the house and have some fun. Finally, on Friday, I got a call from Yvonne.

"What's up, Yvonne?" I said plopping down on the couch.

"Not much. I didn't see you in school today. Were you there?"

"Yeah, I had to take a few make-up tests."

"So, I guess you're trying to kill me with suspense. Are you going to Teen Church with me or not?"

Oooh, I like my women aggressive, I thought with a smile.

"Yeah, I'm going. I didn't know my presence mattered to you all like that. Feels good." I flirted.

When I was met with silence on Yvonne's end of the phone, my smile grew even wider. *I bet she's stunned I'm flirting with her.*

I continued. "My grandmother said it's cool, but she'd like to speak to your mother first. We won't have to go through this every time, but right now, I have to earn her trust back."

"Not a problem. One second, Caleb. Let me grab my mom."

"All right, I'll get my grandmother. Hold on." I stepped into the hallway. "Hey, Gram! My friend Yvonne's mom is on the phone."

"Okay, what's her name, Caleb?"

"Mrs. Jenkins."

She picked up the line and I listened in on my end. "Hello, Mrs. Jenkins? How ya doin', honey? I'm Caleb's grandmother, Lois."

"Hi Miss Lois, I'm fine. I just wanted to let you know that Yvonne will be going to Teen Church on Saturday and she invited Caleb to be her guest."

"That's just fine. Caleb told me that we belong to the same church. What service do you attend? We go to the ten o' clock service."

"Yeah, we must barely miss each other, Miss Lois. We go to the 8 a.m. service but we always hang out for a little while after, talking and catching up with members of the congregation."

"Oh okay. And I always come a bit early, so we have likely been in the same space and didn't know it. Are you on any of the ministries at the church?"

"Yes, Mrs. Jenkins. I usher every second and fourth Sunday."

"That's good. I'm a greeter on first and third Sundays. Hopefully, I'll catch you in church one day."

"That sounds good. I'll be picking Caleb up at six-thirty on Saturday. Nice talking with you, Miss Lois."

"Same here, Mrs. Jenkins. Have a good evening."

"Caleb!" Grandma called, as she hung up the phone. I hurriedly hung up the phone, then headed down the hall. "This young lady really likes you," she said when I entered the room.

"Yeah, she's a good friend of mine. Her mom and dad are nice people."

"It's wonderful to have female friends, so always be sure to treat her with respect. When you go out with her, make sure you always open the door and be courteous."

I smiled at my grandmother's attempt to give me dating advice. It was cute. "Thanks for the tips, Grandma. I'll remember what you told me."

A few minutes later, the doorbell rang. I wondered who it could be for almost nine at night.

"Who is it?" my Grandmother called out, going toward the door.

"It's Mark. Is Caleb home?"

Grandma opened the door. "Yes Mark, but he's on punishment."

He reached out and gave my grandmother a hug. "Nice to meet you, Ms. Lois. I'll only be a minute. I just want to return a game I borrowed from him and tell him something real quick."

Grandma gave him a wary eye before saying, "Okay, Mark. But you can only stay for fifteen minutes."

"Thanks, Ms. Lois." Mark spoke to her back as she quickly left the room.

We walked toward the family room while Mark whispered to me, "Man, your grandma ain't feelin' me, is she?"

"Hmm, I wonder what reason she would have for that," I replied facetiously.

He shrugged. "No clue. Parents normally love me. So, C, are we good for the party?"

"Yeah but check this out. I'm going to church with Yvonne at seven p.m. and at eight p.m., I'm going to have you pick me up."

"Okay, but what if your grandmother finds out?"

"Let me worry about that. She's not going to find out anything. I have it all under control."

"All right, you got it, C. I need to get home and finish my English paper. I'll see you later."

As I closed the door behind him, I began questioning if it was worth it to lie to Grandma about going to the party. I felt bad for taking advantage of her trust in me. The only reason she was allowing me to attend church was for me to get to know God and I was misleading her.

Chapter Eight

The next morning, I found myself scrambling to get to the barber shop. It opened at nine. When I arrived at nine-fifteen, there were already two guys ahead of me. I sat and watched ESPN while I waited. When the conversation in the barber shop turned to the Browns, they caught my attention. Despite their struggles, they would always be my favorite team. Larry, one of the barbers, was a devoted Steelers fan. Every week during football season, he had something bad to say about my team, going on and on until the whole barber shop joined in on the conversation. He got roasted. It was Browns Town.

Finally, it was my turn in the chair.

I sat down and said, "What's good, Gerald?"

"It's slow motion, Caleb. My condolences, man." He stepped around to dap me up and asked, "You good?"

I nodded. "Thanks, man. Yeah, I'm getting there."

"One day at a time, bro," he said. "Same cut?"

"Yeah."

"How's your grandma doing?"

"She's good. Can you look out on the cut today? Got a date tonight." I confessed, more than ready to lighten the mood.

"Oh yeah?" Gerald chuckled. "Where y'all going?"

"She invited me to Teen Church."

"Oh, you got a good girl. And one who knows what she wants. How you meet her?"

"School."

"All right, here's the important question," George said, starting on my lineup.

"Yeah?"

"She cold?"

I smiled. "Most definitely."

"Ha-ha! My man," Gerald stepped around and dapped me up again. "How old is she?"

"We're the same age, seventeen."

"Well, congrats. You're a late bloomer, but you still deserve it," he joked. "Besides, you've been through a lot lately."

"Thanks, G. I appreciate it. You've been my friend and barber ever since I was ten years old."

"Oh yeah. It's all love over here, man."

I remained as still as possible as the clippers trimmed my hair. The sound and the feeling were so soothing that I soon fell asleep.

Before I knew it, I heard, "All right, Caleb. You're all good, my man."

"That was fast." I stretched, then looked in the mirror and said, "Nice job, bro."

After waiting for the bus for almost an hour, I finally made it home, and Grandma and her friend from church were drinking coffee at the kitchen table.

We exchanged greetings and she asked, "You remember my friend, Mrs. Russell?"

"Yes, I do. You read that nice poem at Mom and Dad's funeral, ma'am."

She smiled and nodded. "Yes, that was me."

"It's nice to see you again, Mrs. Russell and thank you for your kind words."

"You too, Caleb. It was my pleasure. I'll print out the poem and have it framed for you."

I smiled warmly. "Thank you, ma'am."

As I left the room, I overheard Grandma telling her that I was such a good boy and that I didn't give her any trouble. I wondered how she would feel after that night. I hoped that she wouldn't find anything out and I could continue to stay under the radar. That was the only way to be while in her house. I looked at my watch and realized it was almost five. I had about an hour and a half to get myself together before Yvonne and her mother would arrive to pick me up.

After showering, washing my hair and ironing my clothes, I was dressed and ready. My grandmother had temporarily given me my phone back and I received a text and saw it was Yvonne.

On my way. She said. *Be there in 5.*

I text back: *Just you?*

I sprayed some cologne on my chest. My phone pinged again. *Yes, driving my sister's car.*

I text back: *Okay, I see you. How long have you had your license?*

About a year and a half. I can teach you, if you want.

Oh, I already have mine. I had my own car, too, but... I stopped typing as my thoughts went to the mangled heap of metal that was my car. It was so badly wrecked after the accident that the insurance company totaled it out and sent a check for the value of the car.

After a few moments, I snapped out of it and deleted the original reply. *Dope. See you soon.*

With shaky hands, I tried to finish getting myself together before Yvonne arrived.

Yvonne pulled up and honked the horn out in the driveway.

"Caleb, I think Yvonne's mother is out there blowing for you," Grandma said, stepping into my room.

"Okay, I'm out. I'll be back by eleven."

She looked at me for a moment, then said, "Have a good time. I love you, and always be aware of your surroundings. Come here and give me a hug." She pulled me into a tight embrace.

Just as I was going out the door, she said, "Caleb?"

I sighed. "Yes?"

"You are such a handsome young man and your haircut looks very nice. Go enjoy yourself. You're not on punishment any longer." Her eyes glistened.

"Thanks, Gram. I'll see you later." I said, pulling my coat collar up as I stepped outside. I couldn't feel any guiltier.

I slid into the car with Yvonne. "Hey, Von."

She smiled and turned down the radio. "What's up, Caleb? Ready to go get lit for Christ?"

I looked over at her goofy grin and

chuckled. "You're too silly, man. Yes, let's do this."

She waved at my grandmother in the window before backing out of the driveway. "I'm glad things worked out. I was a little nervous that she wouldn't let you go. But, maybe she figured you need some JC in your life."

I nodded. "Absolutely. This is the place I need to be, for real."

She looked over at me for a moment. "That's really messed up, what happened. I heard about how your friends curved you and left you holding the bag, literally. Not cool."

I looked out the window, not wanting to speak badly about my friends, but knowing she had a point.

She continued. "I mean, I know you and Mark have been friends a long time, but would a true friend really leave you hanging like that?"

I sighed. "Man, I don't know, Von. It seemed like..."

She waited a few seconds and then asked, "Like what?"

"Like... like they had already discussed all of it before they even picked me up." I chewed my nail anxiously. "I mean, I've known Mark for a very long time, but George and Pete have only been around us for a few months. Mark got closer to them while playing on the football team. They seem cool, but I've definitely noticed a big change in Mark since they've come around. The Mark I've always known would have never allow that to go down."

Yvonne nodded, her eyes on the road. "Yeah, I feel you. As you know, I moved here last year. Mark was one of the first people I met here. I've definitely seen a change in his attitude and behavior lately."

I shook my head. "Yeah, whatever it is, I can't let it continue to affect me. I have my own problems to worry about."

Yvonne reached over and squeezed my hand. "Right. Speaking of that, how have you been? Like, really."

"I've been good overall. I mean, I have my moments, every now and then. It's all still so new..." I trailed off.

She nodded again. "Mmm-hmm. I can't even imagine, Caleb. I just can't."

About ten minutes later, we arrived at the church. The parking lot was full, so we parked down the street and take a shuttle bus over to the church. The place was packed. We walked farther into the sanctuary and I saw some of my friends from school and my neighborhood swaying, lifting their hands, and praising God.

It was interesting to see so many people my age singing and dancing to gospel music. Shortly thereafter, the pastor spoke about us keeping ourselves pure and remaining virgins. But I was way too excited about the upcoming party to fully listen to his message. I glanced at my watch and realized it was almost eight. It was time to make my move.

"Hey, Von?"

"Yeah, Caleb?"

"Can I get past you? I missed a call from home and I need to find out what's going on. I'll be back in a minute."

Once I was outside the sanctuary, I called Mark and told him to come get me.

"Okay, I'll be there in ten minutes," he said. "Be out front."

"Okay. See ya."

I waited a few more minutes, then walked back and took my seat next to Yvonne.

"Everything all right at home?"

"Yes, but I have to leave. My grandmother said my uncle sprained his back while moving some furniture from her bedroom."

I watched her eyes widen. "Oh, that's too bad."

"Yeah, I was really enjoying myself too. But I gotta head out."

"Well... do you need a ride home?"

"No. My grandma is on her way now. I'm just going to wait for her by the front door, so she doesn't have to come inside."

"That's too bad about your uncle. I hope he feels better."

"Me, too. Thanks, Von. And there *will* be a next time. Text me later. I'm not on punishment anymore, so we won't have to sneak around anymore." I winked at her.

She giggled. "Okay. Later, Caleb."

I looked outside and saw Mark waiting for me in the circular driveway. I looked over my shoulder before hopping in. When we were half a block away from the church, Mark turned up the music and I shouted, "It's party time!"

Finally, after a couple wrong turns, we reached Michelle's development. Most of my friends from school were parking or walking up with us. Inside, girls and guys were dancing, and the DJ's playlist was on point.

"Here's the birthday girl," Mark said as we walked up.

I reached out to her for a hug. "Wow, Michelle. You're lookin' good. Happy birthday, girl."

She beamed and did a twirl in her sequin strapless top, leggings, and pumps. "Thanks, Caleb."

"Here's a little something for you." I handed her twenty dollars.

"How sweet. You didn't have to! There's plenty of food in the kitchen. Enjoy yourselves, guys," she said, dancing over to greet her next group of guests.

The party was lively. I looked around to see quite a few people I knew laughing, talking, and dancing.

"Hey, C, you want a beer?" Mark asked.

"No thanks, man." I said. *I'm already pushing it, but Grandma would* kill *me if I came home smelling like alcohol,* I thought.

Mark shrugged his shoulders and grabbed a beer. "Hey man, come outside with me for a minute. I want you to meet someone."

Out in the driveway sat a sky-blue Audi A8 with 22-inch chrome rims.

"Dooope. Whose whip is that?"

"It's my dude Big Mike's. He's the biggest codeine dealer in Cleveland. But don't tell him I told you that," he said.

I nodded, thinking of all the references

I had heard in songs and on TV about the drug.

"Hey, what's up, Mike?"

Mark walked up and dapped up the older teenager.

"What's good, Mark?"

"This is my boy, C."

"Ay, what's good, man?"

"Everything's cool. Just living my best life. I've heard good things about you from Mark. What can I do for you, C?"

"Well, you can start by telling me how I can get a car like that," I joked.

Mike chuckled. "It takes hard work and hustle. When you're serious about making some real money, give me a call."

I raised an eyebrow. "What kind of money are we talking about?"

He smirked. "A stack a week."

"A thousand a week, starting off? Well, that sounds pretty darn good to me!"

They both laughed at my reaction.

"Well, Mark has my number. I've gotta get going, C. Think about it. Peace, y'all."

I stared into space, daydreaming as Mike walked off.

Mark nudged me. "So, what you think, C?"

"That dude has it going on, Mark, but I think I'm going to find a legit part-time gig."

Mark nodded. "That's cool. But when you're ready to make some real paper, let me know. I'll set it up for you."

We talked, laughed, and grabbed something to eat. After a while, I looked at my phone to see if Yvonne had text me. I was horrified when I saw the time was 11:30.

"Aw man, I straight lost track of time. Hurry up, you gotta drop me off. I was supposed to be home at eleven and I know I'm going to have to hear it when I get home, man. I *just* got off punishment."

Mark shook his head. "Man, you'll be eighteen this year. You're not a baby anymore. Just tell her you were dancing and having fun at the party and forgot about what time it was."

"Yeah, that's what I'll tell her. The only problem is I'm not even supposed to be at this stupid party!" I snapped, my voice full of sarcasm.

"I missed four calls. Yvonne called at ten and ten-thirty, and my grandmother at eleven and quarter after eleven. My phone was still on silent from church. I hoped and prayed that Yvonne didn't call the house phone when she didn't get me."

"Does she know the number?" he asked as we headed to his car.

"Yeah. She had to call my grandmother when you guys curved me at the mall last week."

Mark laughed. "Why you bringing up old stuff?"

I just stared at him, salty. "And if Yvonne did tell her, I'm going to let my grandmother know I'm not a child anymore and she needs to respect that I'll be eighteen in a few months. If my parents thought it was fine, I should still be able to stay out until midnight. Besides, when I turn eighteen, I'll be making my own decisions."

"Yeah and I'll help you remove her foot from your behind when you're all done." Mark laughed.

"Look Mark, this is serious. I have to handle my business like a man. Give me a call tomorrow." I said as he dropped me off in front of my house.

"All right, man. See you."

Despite the big talk I had just been doing earlier, I was a little nervous as I slid my key into the lock of the front door. Sweat popped up my forehead and I started to wonder if it was all worth the trouble. I knew it was the moment of truth and I had to face any consequences that may be coming my way. All the lights in the house were off. Hoping not to wake Grandma, I gently walked down the basement stairs to go to the bathroom. That's when she called me.

"Caleb... Caleb?"

"Yeah, Gram?"

"It's midnight. Where in the world have you been, boy?"

I walked into her bedroom and flipped on the light. "I went to church with Yvonne and then I went to a party."

"To a party! You didn't ask me if you could go to a party."

"That's because I knew you would trip. Look, Gram, I really needed this. Ever since Mom and Dad died, I haven't been able to have any real fun."

"I understand that, Caleb, but the bottom line is you disobeyed me. And you lied."

"I didn't lie. I'm telling you the truth."

"You are lying, Caleb Farnsley. Yvonne called here. You lied to her also. She asked about your uncle. When I asked her for more information, she clammed up and said she would talk to you later. I'm guessing you lied about something happening to him, so you could leave the church and go to the party. Right?"

Busted. "Yeah, Gram."

"If you wanted to go to the party, you should have had the decency to ask. But you decided to use people to lie about it. On top of that, you were an hour late coming home. I tried to call you, but you didn't answer. I don't know what to think about all of this right now, but I'll deal with it in the morning. Goodnight."

"But listen, Grandma. I'm a senior in high school, almost eighteen... an adult. I need more freedom."

"I'll give you more freedom once you earn it." "That's fine. When I turn eighteen, I'll just move back in my parents' house, so I won't have to worry about all these rules."

"Boy, are you threatening me? Because you can leave right now."

"I think I'll do just that."

"Caleb, you'd better watch what you say."

"I'm tired of jumping through all of your hoops. I appreciate everything you've done for me, but you're just too strict."

She took a deep breath, then closed her eyes. "Son, I am your grandmother, not your friend. If you are going to live here, you've got to live by my rules."

"In a few months, I'll be the one to making the rules."

"Well, if that's the attitude you're going to take, I guess you can no longer live here." She folded her arms across her chest.

Without another word, I grabbed my backpack, threw in some clothes and my phone and left.

Chapter Nine

I didn't have anywhere to go, so I just wandered the streets for a couple of hours. When I grew tired of that, I called Mark. The phone rang about six times. Finally, he answered in a low, raspy voice.

"Mark, it's me, Caleb."

"What is it, man? I just drifted off to sleep."

"I need to crash at your house for a few days. My grandmother asked me to leave."

"Bruh, do you know what time it is?"

I sighed. "Please, Mark. You more than owe me. I need you to look out."

He paused. "Tonight is fine, but I'll have to check with Mom Dukes about the rest of the time."

"That's fine. I'll be there in about ten minutes."

"All right. Come to the back door."

On Sunday morning, I woke up and realized I was on my own. Relief washed over me. I didn't have to go sit in church all day. Mark's mom cleaned his bedroom and his sisters cleaned the kitchen, so the only thing he did was take out the trash – as it should be.

"You guys want pancakes or waffles this morning?"

"Pancakes please, Ms. Meyers."

I answered.

"So Caleb, tell me what happened between you and your

grandmother," she said as she pulled eggs out of the fridge.

"Ms. Meyers, if it's all right with you, I'd rather talk about it after breakfast."

"That's fine."

After breakfast, Mark and I got on the PlayStation, then chilled watching TV. We walked down the hallway back to Mark's room.

"Yo, C," Mark said. "Your phone's ringing."

"That's just my grandmother. She has nothing new to say to me right now. She's the one that put me out."

"Don't worry, C. My mom said you could crash here for as long as you need to."

"That's what's up. Thanks for looking out."

"Yeah, you know there's nothing I won't do for you."

"Let me check my messages. I put in an application at Walmart and the manager finally called me for an interview."

Mark shut his bedroom door and asked me, "Man, why do you want to work at Walmart for that chump change when you could be making one thousand dollars a week working for Mike?"

"That's not for me, man."

"Do you see that car he's driving, man? All you have to do is take a package to its owner, collect the money, and leave it."

"Sounds real simple, but it's too dangerous. Besides, I got lucky last time with that judge throwing my case out and I don't want to get caught up in anything else." There was a knock at the door, causing us to jump.

"Yeah?"

"It's me, Mark," Ms. Meyers said. "I need to speak with Caleb."

"Yes, Ms. Meyers, here I come." I said,

getting up from the bed.

"Let's go into the den." We walked into the back room and sat on the loveseat. "Before you say anything, I just got off the phone with your grandmother. I called to let her know you were here. She knows that you're safe, but I have to tell you, she's disappointed and angry with you."

"I know, Ms. Meyers. I said some things I wish I could take back."

"Caleb, she said it wasn't the things you said, but your actions that caused her to feel disrespected. She feels like you gave no consideration to her feelings when she was up worried and waiting for you to come home."

"That wasn't my intention. I love my grandmother, but sometimes she treats me just like a little kid."

"How so?"

"Always nagging me to do chores, invading my personal space, always pushing her religious beliefs on me. It's always, 'Caleb... you have to go church... Jesus this and Jesus that... And quoting scripture after scripture. I am just tired of it."

"I understand how you feel, Caleb. You're used to being at home with your parents, and any new living environment is going to take some adjustment. But your grandmother loves you and she's only trying to help you. I know you're a little frustrated and angry, but please patch things up with her. She won't hesitate to forgive you because she truly loves you."

"I know. Like I said, I do feel bad about how it all went down."

"God has already forgiven you, but you have to forgive yourself. That was the past. The question is, what are you going to do about it now?"

"I know I need to apologize and get myself together."

"Sounds good. I can take you home, where you belong."

"Thanks for letting me crash here for a night."

"Anytime, Caleb. Hopefully, the next time will be under better circumstances."

I smiled and said, "I'm sure it will."

That evening, Mark and his mother took me home. When we pulled into the driveway, I saw my grandma waiting by the door with open arms, ready to embrace me. I could feel the love she had for me when I looked into her eyes. The closer I got to her, the more my emotions began to shift. Tears flowed down my face as I became overwhelmed by all the pain I'd experienced recently.

"I'm so sorry, Gram. I didn't mean what I said to you. Please forgive me."

"I forgive you. Forgive me too, Caleb."

After we waved goodbye to Mark and his mom, I opened the door and was greeted by the aroma of a hot Sunday dinner.

"Mmm, Grandma, what's that you're cooking? It smells good."

"I made your favorite dish - cabbage, red-skinned potatoes, and Italian sausage with homemade cornbread. And, for dessert, key lime pie."

I turned to look at her. "Why would you cook all that for me when I've put you through all this?"

"My love for you is not based on conditions of whether you are good today or bad tomorrow. John fifteen and seventeen says we are commanded by Jesus our Lord and Savior, to love one, regardless of how we act. So, no matter what you do, I am going to love you with all my heart. But we still need to talk. Why don't you take your backpack and clothes into your room and I'll fix your plate? Then we can discuss a few things."

Soon after grandma blessed the table, silence fell in the kitchen. Nothing was moving but my fork and knife. Then Grandma said, "Son, is it true? Do you think I treat you like a child?"

"Grandma, I didn't mean it exactly like that." She shook her head. "No, son, just keep it one hundred with me."

I smiled. It was funny to hear my grandmother use slang phrases. "I am keeping it real with you. The main problem I have with living here is that you're always trying to force religion on me. Please understand, I would like to know God for myself. I know you mean well, but please respect that it needs to be in my own time."

"Caleb, what's going to happen when you leave for college and you don't have me to talk to? What are you going to do then?"

I chuckled. "I don't know, Grandma. Make some friends?"

"Son, don't laugh because it's not funny. I just want you to know that the Lord is watching over you. He takes care of fools and babies and you're acting very foolish right now. Stealing, lying, breaking curfew... Caleb, you've always been a well-behaved boy. I know you're still coping with your parents' death. But the devil is real and his assignment is to destroy your life."

I rolled my eyes. "Here we go again with this spooky stuff."

"Son, listen to me. I love you and I just want the best for you. But as long as you live in this house, you have to obey my rules. They're non-negotiable."

"Grandma, I apologize to you again for what I said and for the way I have been acting. I totally disrespected you with my actions and words and for that, I'm truly sorry. But can you tell me one thing?

"What is it?"

"How can I defeat the devil?"

"That's easy. Romans ten and nine says, accept Jesus Christ as your Lord and Savior. Your whole life needs to be committed to Him.

After you accept Him, He will give you the gift of the Holy Spirit to live inside you. The spirit of the Lord will help and guide you."

"But Grandma, how will I know if the spirit is really there?"

"John eight and thirty-six says, when Jesus died for you, He set you free to live by following the Spirit. If you walk by the Spirit, you will receive eternal life." She lifted her hands. "Hallelujah, praise God, from whom all blessings flow! Boy, you're going to make me shout in here."

I watched the tears well in her eyes. "Gram, you're scaring me."

"I just hope and pray that one day you will love the Lord as much as I do. Caleb, with all the things that I have been through over the years, I can't help but give Him praise and glory."

"That's good. Maybe you can talk to Him about me, so I can become a better person."

"Son, I *always* pray for you, but you must believe that He will make you a better person."

"Grandma, can we make up and start fresh?"

"Yes, we can, Caleb. But remember, you will need to obey my rules and respect me at all times. And one more thing, son. You're back on punishment for a week."

"But Grandma, I thought we were going to start fresh." I joked.

"Nice try, Caleb. I forgive you, but there are still consequences for your actions. And I'm really taking it easier on you than I should."

I shrugged. "I guess you're right. I'm going to do better from now on. And I've made up my mind to listen to your advice. I could use your wisdom right about now."

"That's good. I won't tell you anything wrong. I love you and I want the best for you. First Peter five and eight says, 'keep yourself out of harm's way because the devil is looking for someone to devour'. He wants you, but he can't have you because you don't belong to him. You are God's child and He loves you dearly, Caleb. So, stay encouraged."

"I will, Grandma."

"Well, I don't know about you, but that food has made me sleepy. What time is it?"

"It's almost nine and I have to get ready for school tomorrow. What a weekend."

"Who are you telling? Look downstairs on the table. I washed and folded all your clothes."

"Thanks, Gram. I love and appreciate you more than words can express."

"I love you, too. Remember, love lasts forever."

On Monday morning, I awakened to nature's alarm clock of birds singing and chirping right outside my window. For a few minutes, I just lay there, not wanting to get up. Then my grandmother called up to tell me she had made a small breakfast for me.

"Thanks, Gram," I said, once I got downstairs. "I'm running a little late, but I'll make it to school on time."

"You'll be just fine. I went outside for a walk this morning and the weather is just beautiful. It's about seventy degrees out there. You should ride your bike to school."

I told her it was a good idea, and after a hearty breakfast, I was off to class. The sun beamed, and the spring breeze felt great. I felt good about myself.

That's when I rode up on Mark and Big Mike who sat in the car, talking to Yvonne. Seeing them together almost made me sick to my stomach. At first, I tried to act like I didn't see them. To my surprise, Mark called me over.

"Yo, what's up, C?" He smiled. "I see you've got wheels today!"

"And I see you got jokes today. I'm trying to make it to class a little early. I need to see my science teacher. I'll see y'all later." I turned my back to ride toward the school and Yvonne's voice, louder than I'd ever heard it, stopped me in my tracks.

"Is Mark the only one you see?"

"Hey, Mike. Hey, Yvonne. I was going to speak."

Mike nodded his greeting.

Yvonne crossed her arms. "Yet another lie."

My cheeks flushed. "I'll talk to you later."

"What's wrong with you, Mr. Caleb Farnsley?

You act like you have an attitude today."

So aggressive, and she's calling out my government name? I thought. "Naw, I don't. I have to go see my science teacher before the bell rings. I've got about ten minutes. I'll see you in fourth period."

"Fine, Caleb."

She was right about my attitude. Her talking to Mark and Big Mike made me jealous. But I couldn't let any of them know. After all, Yvonne and I were just friends. But I wanted to be more than friends. I wanted to protect her from guys like Big Mike, who used money and gifts to get women. I was also a little annoyed with her for not covering me when I left church early on Saturday. But realized I had no valid reason to feel that way. I'd put myself in that situation by the choices I made. Besides, that caused Grandma and me to have that great talk and get some clarity, so it all happened for a reason.

All morning long, I sat in class, thinking about making things right with Yvonne. My attention span was very short, and I often drifted away in my thoughts. My mind raced as I tried to think of the best way to ask her to prom. I wrote her a note to test the waters and passed it to her in the hallway. She responded and passed it to me in the hall during the next class change. We finally made up, after what seemed like an eternity, during fourth period. It was lunchtime.

Taco salad was on the menu. I sat close to the entrance of the cafeteria and waited patiently so she would see me. Five minutes passed, and I was cool. Ten minutes later, I was anxious. After fifteen minutes, I grew nervous. Twenty minutes later, I felt annoyed again.

I couldn't take it anymore. I walked out to the common area reserved for seniors, only to find her eating lunch by herself.

"Ay, I've been looking for you. I thought we were going to meet up and talk."

She slowly looked up at me and, for the second time that day, she wasn't wearing her trademark smile. "We have ten minutes before we go back to class, Caleb. Start talking."

I was taken aback by her sassiness. *Once again, I love that aggressive side of her!* I thought as I tried to put my words together.

"Yvonne, I have a confession I need to make to you."

"Yeah?"

I reached into my book bag and pulled out a small Krispy Kreme box with a note attached that said, *Please donut say no. Will you go to prom with me?* "I would like to take you to prom."

Her face finally lit up with the smile I'd grown to love. "Of course, Caleb Farnsley. I thought you'd never ask." She reached into her book bag and handed me a package of Pop Rocks with a note attached that said, *I'm so glad you* popped *the question. Prom would rock with you as my date.*

"Wow, Yvonne! You've made my day, my week, my month, and my year."

"Come here, boy. Heart you forevs!" She grabbed me, and we made it official with a warm hug. We took a selfie and pictures of the notes and posted them on Instagram. I heard a couple of catcalls in the distance and blushed.

"That's the bell. Write me a note!" she rushed off to her next class.

For the next two hours, all I could do was smile because Yvonne and I were going to prom together. When school let out, I found myself rushing to get home, so I could tell Grandma the good news.

Chapter Ten

I breezed in the door. Grandma sat at the kitchen table with a cup of tea. "Hey, Caleb. How was school?"

"I had a wonderful day. As a matter-of-fact, I have some good news."

"That's funny. I have some good news to tell you, also."

"You go first, Gram."

"No, you can go first, Caleb."

"Okay. I asked Yvonne to go to prom with me and she said yes," I told her, beaming.

"Congratulations, son! I knew she would."

"Thanks, Gram. So, what's your good news?"

"Well, John three and sixteen tells us that God so loved the world, that He gave His only begotten son, that whoever believes in him shall not perish but have eternal life!"

"Yeah, I guess God's been good to me because Yvonne's going to prom with me despite me acting like a knucklehead, like Dad would say."

We both laughed.

"That's wonderful, Caleb, but I have more good news."

"What is it, Gram?"

"The manager from Walmart called and he wants to know what day you can come in for an interview."

"Thank you, Jesus! What a day!" Grandma lifted a brow and I laughed at her reaction.

"I can't deny that God is good. I really need this job to help me pay for prom and my senior dues. God has really blessed me, so I'm more than thankful."

"You go, boy! I mean, *man* of god. I am proud of you, Caleb. Whatever you do in life, always put God first. Matthew six and thirty-three says, 'Seek the kingdom and its righteousness and all things will be added unto you'. Son, always obey Him and He will take care of you." She placed her hand on my shoulder. "Look at me, I am a living witness. He didn't let me get this old for nothing. But you know something? I don't feel eighty-three years old. I have a few aches and pains, but every time I read His word, it's like I am being renewed in my spirit. The pages leap into my heart and the feeling I get – I can't even describe it. It's like I am being filled with something only God can give me and sometimes it makes me cry and shout at the same time. Praise the Lord! Praise the Lord."

"Wow, Grandma. If it makes you feel like that, I want to try it."

"Caleb, the time is now. Give your life to Him because He loves you."

I nodded. "You're right, Gram. Everything has been going downhill since I learned that my parents died. I'm not making good choices and I've felt so empty. I just need to give my life to Him."

My grandmother choked up at my confession. "Son, when you do that, you will never be the same. Your whole life will change."

"I want to change. What can I do?"

"Son, Romans ten and nine says that 'if you confess with your mouth that Jesus is Lord and believe in your heart that God raised Him from the dead, you will be saved'."

"That's all I gotta do to be saved, Gram?"

She nodded. "Yes, just believe."

"I do believe. I confess Jesus is Lord and I believe God raised Him from the dead." I blinked. "So, am I saved now?"

"Yes, my dear. You are. Second Corinthians five and seventeen says that 'if anyone is in Christ he is a new creature. The old things are passed away. Behold all things are new'," she said, quoting from memory.

"So, are you saying that I'm a new person?"

"Yes, you are, son. When you confessed the

Good News, God adopted you into the family of believers and you have now become one of His children."

I nodded, still processing how simple it was. "But what if I mess up and do something wrong?"

"Caleb, you won't be perfect just because you accepted Jesus as your Savior. As you read your Bible every day and pray, the Holy Spirit, which lives inside you, will help you live the way God wants you to."

"And another thing, Caleb." She beamed with pride. "You are now a candidate for baptism."

"Is that when the pastor dips you into the water?"

"Yes. Being baptized with water for the forgiveness of your sins by the Father, Son, and the Holy Spirit, like in Matthew twenty-eight and nine, shows that you're acknowledging publicly that you are a part of Christ's family, the church. So now you have to be on alert."

"Alert for what?"

"You belong to God and the devil doesn't like it. He tells us in Ephesians six and eleven that He's going to do all he can to try to destroy you, but God has given us weapons to fight him. Not weapons like guns or knives, but spiritual weapons, such as putting the belt of truth around your waist and the protection of righteous living up on your chest."

"Okay... that sounds pretty dope."

Grandma continued. "On your feet, you will wear the good news of peace to help you stand strong. And, also use the shield of faith, which can stop all the burning arrows of the devil. Accept God's salvation as your helmet and take the sword of the spirit, which is the word of the Lord. Son, don't ever forget these things."

She got up and pulled a white, leather-bound Bible from the drawer.

"Hebrews four and twelve tells us that the Bible is alive and well. People will walk away from you and leave you, but Jesus will always be there. He says in His word that He will never leave you, nor forsake you. Your mother and father had to leave you, but the Lord took you in. Amen."

"Thank you, Gram, for always giving me your encouraging words. I know that I've resisted listening for all this time, but I really appreciate you, and I thank God in heaven that you're my grandmother."

"Aww, come over here, son. Give me a big hug. I appreciate you too, Caleb. I've really enjoyed your company over these past few months and I'm glad you chose to live here with me. I'm getting older and I can't do the things I used to do, so I need a strong young man like yourself to help me out. It goes both ways. You need me, and I need you. We need each other."

"I guess you're right, Grandma. We need each other, but right now, I need a job. Let me call Walmart to find out what time they want me to come in for the interview."

"Go right ahead, Caleb. The job is already yours. Just claim it by faith, then put some action behind your faith and things will work out for you."

"Thank you. I love you." Still in her embrace, I kissed her cheek.

"I love you too, Caleb. Always remember, if you believe it you can achieve it."

"Amen to that, Grandma."

It turned out the store manager wanted to interview me the same day. I put on a shirt and tie and called Uncle Cal to take me there.

When I got into the car, he looked over at me and smiled. "Caleb, you look very handsome."

I smiled. "Thanks, Uncle Cal. I'm pretty nervous."

"Don't worry, everything will go just fine. Hey, I'm going to make this short and sweet, because as you know, I'm a man of few words."

I nodded, waiting to hear what he had to say.

"When your parents were here, I admit, I didn't play as active of a role in your life that I should have as your uncle. We would see each other at Thanksgiving and Christmas, but I didn't take the time to spend quality time with you."

I shook my head. "That's okay, Uncle Cal. I knew how busy you were with your career. Mom would always talk about your business trips."

He waved my response off. "Still... no excuse. But that's all going to change right now. You're my nephew and you need a father figure in your life. I will happily take on that responsibility because I love you."

I cringed. *The last time a man told me he loved me, I lost him forever,* I thought about my Dad.

"I promise, I will be here for you whenever you need me and even when you don't. I'm not looking to replace your Dad, because I never could. But I do want to try to fill some of the void he left in your life."

I sniffed, and my throat hurt as I held back my tears. Why in the world were we having this emotional conversation right before my interview? It was much needed, but I needed to get my head right. "Thanks, Uncle Cal. That means a lot to me."

He nodded, while wiping his eye. "Whatever happened to your involvement with the track team? You used to be so into that."

I lowered my head fiddled with my hands. "I don't know. I guess I figured no one would care if I stopped training."

"Why would you say that?"

"Pops was the only one who came to my meets. That was our thing, so he would be at all of them. Now, there's no one there to root me on in the stands, so what's the use?"

I could see a myriad of emotions pass over Uncle Cal's face as he focused on the road ahead.

A few moments of silence passed before he spoke again. "Caleb, I vow to come to every meet, game, match, rally or anything else you're involved in, from here on out. That includes the rest of your high school and college careers."

I thought I saw a tear drop off the left side of his face, but I couldn't be sure. It really touched me to know that Uncle Cal really cared that much about me. I felt my eyes start to burn but I still refused to let a tear fall. I'd already done more than enough crying over the past couple of months. I held my right fist out and smiled when my Uncle thumped his against it. That was our unspoken vow and nothing else needed to be said.

After my talk with Uncle Cal, I began to feel a lot better about my interview. I'd been nervous before, but once I said a quick prayer, the fear immediately melted away.

I entered the store and walked up to the customer service desk. "Hello. My name is Caleb Farnsley and I'm here for a job interview with Tim, the store manager."

"Hi, I'm Rose Mary, the front-end manager and it's nice to meet you. I'll get Tim, for you. Just a moment."

As Rose Mary picked up the phone, a big dude approached me and said, "Are you Caleb Farnsley?"

"Yes, sir."

"You're early. You get points for punctuality." He then introduced himself as Tim and asked if I was ready for the interview.

"Yes. I am, sir."

We began walking toward the back of the store.

"I believe I spoke to your grandmother on the phone."

"Yes, sir."

"Well, she seems to be very proud of you. By the way, you don't have to call me sir, just Tim."

We made our way through the door marked *Employees Only* and up a back stairwell.

"Yes, that sounds like her. She's a wonderful lady."

Tim nodded. "I'm sure. Well, here's my office. Have a seat and we can get this started."

After our small talk, I felt completely relaxed with Tim. Everything seemed to be going very well and the more questions he asked, the more my confidence grew. For the first time in a long time, I felt like I was back on the right track to making my parents proud.

After interviewing with the assistant manager, I was offered the job, contingent on me passing the drug and background test.

"Thank you, Jesus," I sighed, walking out of the store. I wasn't nervous about the background check because the judge threw out my shoplifting case a few weeks prior. She had been informed about what happened to my parents, looked at my honor roll report card, read the character letters from my teachers and grief and guidance counselors and took pity on me.

I called my grandmother once I reached the parking lot and she was just as excited.

"Can I start once they finalize my paperwork?"

"Yes, as long as your homework gets done. How many days do they want you to work?"

"Just three. Tuesdays, Thursdays, and Saturdays from four p.m. to nine p.m."

"That's good. Maybe you can work a little more in the summertime before you go off to college. But, for now, you need to concentrate on your schoolwork."

"You're right, Grandma. This is only short-term, to pay for prom, my senior dues, and some of the things I'll need for my dorm. Then I am off to OSU."

"Now that you're going to be making money, you need to open a checking and savings account at the credit union. Also, you should put six percent of your income in Walmart's 401(k) plan to invest."

"Gram, I'm only seventeen years old. I'll have plenty of time to put money away."

"You're right, but the time is always now. That's how your parents were able to take such good care of you. Financial planning and saving.

I forgot to ask you, what department will you be working in?"

"I'm going to stock shelves and load people's cars in the online pickup area. Yup, I'm going to be that guy."

"Son, don't sound so sad. We all have to start somewhere. Colossians three and twenty-three tells us, 'whatever work you do, do it to the best of your ability and do it heartily, as for the Lord rather than for man. Knowing that from the Lord, you will receive the reward of the inheritance.' It is the Lord whom you serve, Caleb. In other words, be the best stocker and loader the world has ever seen."

I smiled. Her pep talk actually made me feel better. I could work hard and always move up, if I chose to stay on with the company once I moved to Columbus. "Amen to that."

I went through a few weeks of training and everything went smoothly. The employees were nice, and I caught on to things quickly. When I received my first paycheck, I was surprised to see it was a nice amount. I was able to take Yvonne out on a couple of dates, treat Grandma to dinner and a movie, and go out with my friends and have some fun.

Chapter Eleven

Life had certainly leveled up for me after the struggle I'd recently experienced. Just a few months prior, I had been mourning the loss of my parents and things looked hopelessly bleak. But God is good, and He knew I'd need someone like Grandma Lois to help me through it all. He set it all up for my good.

I prayed to Him frequently throughout the day with the same prayer. "Thank you, Lord, for all You have done and will do. If you order my steps, I'll praise Your holy name. Amen."

I read the Bible several times a week and I could not put it down. The more I read, the better I felt. It seemed like the Lord was telling me to surrender to Him. I made up my mind that I would follow Christ, get baptized and live my life for Jesus. It was what my parents would want, and it was best for me.

One Sunday afternoon, while at the Word Church, I went down to the altar and became a candidate for baptism. The following week, it was almost my turn to go into the pool and the choir was singing, "Take Me to the Water."

I looked at Grandma, Yvonne, Uncle Cal, and Aunt Shirley. They were all giving me smiles and nods of approval. I felt very nervous and timid. The moment of truth had hit me. I was going down in the water to be buried like Christ, only to rise up and become a new creation. Part of me wished my other friends were also there to see it. But I thought about what Grandma said about having to fight a battle once I accepted Christ.

The actual baptism lasted only a few seconds, to my surprise. While the deacons wiped my face, Yvonne took a picture of me and I heard Grandma and Uncle Cal praising the Lord.

"Come over here and give me a hug. Congratulations, Caleb." Grandma gripped me tightly, unfazed by my wet garments.

"Thank you, Gram."

"Boy, your mother and father would be very proud of you."

I smiled, knowing she was right.

"You're growing up to be a fine young man. Continue to do good and live right. Listen Caleb, now that you belong to the Kingdom of God, that old devil is really going to try to mess with you. Just continue to read your Bible and pray. When you resist him, he will eventually flee."

"Yeah you're right," I nodded. "But right now, Grams, I'm going to get out of these wet clothes. I'll meet y'all in the front of the church in about fifteen minutes."

I met up with everyone after I got dressed, and Gram surprised me by taking us all out to dinner at my favorite restaurant, Red Lobster. I ate more crab legs and cheddar bay biscuits than I could count, with a virgin daiquiri to wash it all down.

"Caleb, I am so proud of you," Uncle Cal said. "You're such a blessing to this family. We've watched in pride as you have matured into a nice young man. Your parents would be proud."

"Thanks, Uncle Cal. I wish that they could be here, but I thank God for you, Grandma, Aunt Shirley and also for you too, Yvonne, for being my rock. All of you are very important to me. Gram, if you hadn't taken me in when mom and dad died, I don't know where I would have ended up. Uncle Cal, you could have let me sit in jail. But, Grandma, you told me about Romans eight and twenty-eight, which says, 'all things work together for the good of those who love the Lord' and I love Him very much. I couldn't see it then, but I see it clearly now. All those setbacks were really a setup for me to join the Kingdom. And God used you to help bring me in. What a great God we serve."

"Listen to my baby quoting scripture!" Grandma shouted.

I shrunk down in the booth, embarrassed at her outburst.

Uncle Cal laughed. "Caleb, you sound like you preachin', boy."

"No, Uncle Cal. Just sharing my testimony. Grandma said your test becomes your testimony and I thought I would just share it with all of you."

I looked over as Grandma beamed with pride. "Ayyy, you was listening." She smiled even wider.

"Praise Him! Yass," Yvonne said, smiling.

"Are there any ministries you would like to join in the church?" Aunt Shirley asked me.

"I wouldn't mind being a youth usher or joining the outreach ministry. But I have twelve weeks of new member classes to complete, then I'll make a decision on what I want to do." I stretched, rubbing my full belly. "I don't know about y'all, but I am stuffed and ready to go. It's been a long day. You tired, Gram? I see you over there dozing off."

"A little bit. This food is weighing on my eyelids and it's almost nine. My program will be on at nine-thirty."

We left the waitress a nice tip and were on our way home when I asked, "Gram, is it cool if we drop Yvonne off first so I can walk her to her door?"

"Yes. You can, Caleb, but don't stay too long. Remember you have school tomorrow and it's getting late."

Grandma, Uncle Cal, and Aunt Shirley said their goodbyes as we pulled into the driveway.

"You know what, Caleb, I am not going to wait for you," Grandma said. "My show will be on in five minutes. You can walk back home."

"All right, Gram. I'll be there in a minute."

Not wanting to waste any time, I quickly walked Yvonne to her door. "Thank you for being a part of this day, Yvonne. It wouldn't have meant the same without you there. Your invitation to Teen Church, studying the Bible with me, and just keeping me encouraged during this hard time has meant a lot."

"No problem, Caleb. Thanks for inviting me. I had such a good time. Your grandmother is hilar. Please tell her I said thanks for the dinner."

I licked my lips, while staring into her eyes. "No problem."

"Caleb, there's something on your eyelash. Close your eyes."

I closed my eyes and was surprised when I felt her warm lips pressed against my cheek.

It was sweet and innocent, but I swear my heart was beating triple time. Goosebumps sprouted all over my skin. I just couldn't believe it. It was my first kiss from a girl and it she had fully taken the reigns.

"Goodnight, Caleb. I'll see you in school tomorrow." She gave a finger wave and winked.

"Goodnight, Yvonne. God bless you."

I smiled all the way home. Yvonne had made me a very happy dude. When I walked in the door, Grandma was watching her show.

"Caleb, is that you?"

"Yeah."

"Come in here and sit with me for a minute." She noticed my smile and asked, "Are you all

right, son?"

"More than all right, Grams."

"Mm-hmmm. And just what has you smiling like that, Caleb?"

My cheeks flushed. "Uhhh...nothing, Gram."

"Yeah, you do know, coming in here all googly-eyed. That girl kissed you and now you've gone crazy."

I was shocked by her response. "How did you know *she* kissed *me*?"

"Boy, I'm eighty years old. I've been there and done that. Remember, I was your age once and I saw the way you've been looking at her. She's a very attractive and classy young lady, so be careful. I know your body is changing and you're becoming a young man. The more you see her, the closer you two will become. Then you may want to try something."

I chuckled. "Liiiike?"

"Like sex."

"Dang, Gram. You're blunt. Naw, I'm waiting until I get married. I only want to share that with the woman the Lord gives me as my wife. I've always felt that way."

"That's right, Caleb. Proverbs eighteen and twenty-two says, 'he that finds a wife finds a good thing', so you will get yours in due season. Just continue to concentrate on the Lord and serve Him. Finish high school and prepare for college."

"That's the course I'm going to take, if the Lord's willing."

"Son, the Lord is always willing but are you able? Just take it one day at a time, Caleb. Let God direct your path. He has promised plans for you, plans for welfare and not for calamity to give you a future and hope. Son, lean and depend on Him. Cast all your problems on Him, because Jesus cares about you."

"Thanks for always encouraging me to do right. I know you've had your work cut out for you, Gram."

"You're welcome. I will always tell you the truth because John eight and thirty-two tells us 'the truth will set you free'. The Word of God is truth, so be careful Caleb to not only listen to what I am saying but to obey it."

"I will. I am a new creation in Christ. I'm gonna let the Spirit guide me from here on out."

"Now you're talking, boy and it sounds good. Listen, it's almost eleven, way past my bedtime. We had a busy day today and the Lord saw us through it. Goodnight, son." She planted a wet kiss on my cheek.

I chuckled. "Goodnight, Gram."

I tossed and turned all night. There was a lot of stuff on my mind, ranging from my mom and dad to Yvonne. It was the middle of the night and suddenly I was compelled to get down on my knees to pray. After getting back in bed, I fell asleep like a baby.

The next morning, I couldn't wait to get to school and see Yvonne. First through fourth periods passed, but she was nowhere in sight. I finally saw her sitting at the table in the lunchroom, talking to Mark.

I walked up and greeted them both. "Hey guys, what's good?"

Yvonne looked up at me and grinned. "Hey. Just talking about prom."

I lifted an eyebrow. "Did you find a date yet, Mark?"

"Nope."

"You better hurry. You only have two more weeks. Hey, maybe you should look on Tinder."

"Yeah, that's real funny, *Caleb*."

"Just a joke, *Mark*."

"Yeah, okay..." he muttered.

"What's up with you, dude?" I asked.

He seemed to lighten up a little. "Nothing. I heard the news. You're very lucky to have Yvonne as your date."

"No, Mark, it's not luck at all. It's God's favor, and favor ain't fair."

He chuckled. "Man, what are you talking about?"

"Favor is when God gives his children good things that they don't expect or deserve."

"I don't know, man, but for the last couple of weeks... you've been changing. I don't know what Kool-Aid your church has you sippin', but you have gotten way too religious on me." Mark shook his head.

I frowned, and Yvonne and I briefly made eye contact. She shook her head, but I ignored her warning and pressed the issue. "Mark, it's not religion. It's my personal relationship with Jesus Christ."

"All right, y'all. I'm outta here. I'll see y'all later." Mark got up and left the cafeteria.

Yvonne gazed at me for a moment. "What was that all about, Caleb?"

"I don't know, Yvonne. Hopefully I just planted a seed that somebody else will water for him. God will get the increase."

She nodded. "Yeah, you're right. He definitely needs Jesus. Why don't we invite him to Teen Church?"

"That sounds like a good idea, Yvonne. Maybe we will have another opportunity to share the love of Christ with him."

"You and Mark have been friends for a long time. Maybe God will use you to get your friend saved by the way he sees you living."

"I hope so. I know I'll have to put work in, but that's my boy and I'm determined to tell him about God." I ate some of the food Grandma packed. "I'm going straight to work after school, so I'll call you on my break."

"Don't forget, Caleb, because you still need to find a tie and new shoes to match my dress. Plus, I need to go over a few other things with you."

"Yes, dear." I joked in monotone. "I won't forget. Talk to you later."

When I arrived at work, I called my grandmother to check in. While walking to the break room to clock in, one of the zone managers, Brian Jones, came up to me and said, "Caleb, I want to let you know that we really appreciate the great work you've done for us so far."

"Thank you, Brian."

"I've been watching the way you interact with the customers and employees. You've also received some favorable feedback on our customer surveys."

"That's great to hear. I really enjoy working here."

He paused for a moment. "Caleb, do you mind if I ask you a personal question?"

I nodded, curious. "Yes, you can ask me anything."

"Are you a Christian?"

I beamed. "Yes, I am, sir, and proud of it."

"I knew it! I knew there was something different about you when I first met you."

"Yeah, I love the Lord and try to show it in my interactions with others. I'm glad to hear He's showing all over me."

"I could tell, and He is. Now that we've learned we're brothers in Christ, we can encourage each other and lift one another up." Brian smiled warmly.

"You're right, Brian. My grandmother always says that iron sharpens iron."

"She's right, Caleb. Next month I'm going to be transferring to a new store in Columbus. I've been promoted to store manager."

"Nice. Congratulations."

"Thanks, Caleb. I know you'll be attending OSU in Columbus in the fall, so if you ever need a job, I'll be sure to look out for you while you're in college or thereafter."

I smiled. "Thanks a lot, Brian. It's a blessing to know good people."

"Same here. Before I leave, let's grab some wings or pizza. Whatever it is, I know we'll both enjoy the fellowship."

"Sounds like a plan, Brian. Let me know when and I'll be there."

He gave me his number and I told him how grateful I was and how much I enjoyed working with him.

"Have a good evening, Caleb. I'll see you tomorrow."

After work, I was very tired and hungry. It was about ten when I got home. Grandma was asleep, but she left me a couple hot dogs and some pork and beans on the stove. By the time I ate dinner and took a shower, it was almost eleven. I looked down at my cell to see Mark was calling.

"What's up, C? Were you asleep?"

"Naw, just about to get on the game for a minute before heading to bed."

"Cool. Ay, I was wondering if you could ride with me tomorrow to pick up a suit for prom."

"Yeah. As long as I'm back before six o' clock because Yvonne and I are going out."

"I thought you guys were just friends."

I felt my eyebrow lift. "We are... but we're vibin' and figuring things out right now."

"Yeah, okay."

"Come on, now. You know the last thing I'm about to do is try to convince you about my platonic nature of my relationship with Yvonne."

Mark chuckled. "Yeah, it would be like trying to talk to a brick wall, because I know you're feeling her."

I rolled my eyes. "Anyway, I'll see you tomorrow, man."

After waking from a good night's rest the next morning, it dawned on me that it was Friday and also payday. I was excited about going to the movies with Yvonne that evening. I hurried and got dressed for school, hoping to see her before class.

Downstairs, I grabbed a banana from the fruit bowl before grabbing my books off the table.

Grandma sipped her morning coffee at the breakfast bar. "Son, why are you in such a rush? You're running fifteen minutes ahead of time. Why don't you fix something to eat before you go?"

"No, thanks. I'm trying to get to school a little early, so I can talk to Yvonne."

"Won't you see her tonight?" "Yeah, Gram, but..."

"Boy, you better eat something, so you can think straight. You can't learn anything on a near-empty stomach."

"Yeah, I guess you're right." I grabbed a bagel to go with my banana. "I'll eat this on the way. Gotta go. Love you."

"Love you, too. See you this afternoon, son. Have a blessed day."

I made a mad dash for school, hoping to see Yvonne before classes started. Just as I was locking up my bike, I spotted Yvonne's dad dropping her off.

We exchanged our usual greetings and then she said, "Caleb, I'm very excited about our date tonight. What movie do you want to go see?"

"I'm not sure. When I'm in study hall I'll look at the Fandango."

She smiled, looking content. "Sounds good."

"By the way, Yvonne. Let's plan to grab a seven-thirty show, then grab Chipotle afterward."

"Okay. My curfew's not until midnight on the weekends, so that's fine."

"Okay. So, I'll see you after class?"

"No, I have a hair appointment. My mom is picking me up, but I'll text you once I get under the dryer."

"Okay, I'm rolling with Mark to pick out his suit for prom, but I should be back around six."

"Cool. Remember, the color is light blue. I'll text you a picture of the fabric swatch. What do you think about matching tees for after prom and Cedar Point?"

"I don't know about that, but we can discuss it later. I have to get to class. Later."

As I turned to head toward my English class, Yvonne stopped me and said, "I'm very happy that you're my friend," and gave me a hug.

She smelled and felt so good, it took me a minute to get my head right afterward. Grandma was right. The more I saw her, the closer we became, and I started to have thoughts about being even closer. I made a vow to stay a virgin until I get married, but my body was feeling one way and my mind was thinking another.

"Lord, please help me," I murmured on my way to class.

After school, Mark was waiting for me by the front entrance.

"Whaddup, C?"

"Nothing, man. Just glad it's Friday so I can sleep in tomorrow. Can you swing me by Walmart to pick up my check after we leave the Men's Store?"

"Yup," Mark said. "I can't wait until the summer. We have only three more weeks before we're finished. We'll be done with school, almost eighteen and ready to have some real fun. Are you still going away to college?"

"Yeah, but I'm not leaving until August eighteenth. Have you thought about what you want to do after school?"

"I'm gonna take the summer off, then I may enroll at Tri-C in the fall."

"Fall sounds good. Any longer than that and you may not want to go back at all."

"Yeah, I'm going back. I just don't know what I want to major in so I'm going to take a break. Caleb, what's up with you, though? You sound like my father, asking me about my life plans."

"Not trying to be pops, so you can chill. I'm just giving my friend some advice."

"Well, since you're my friend, thank you for your advice. Ay, I gotta make a stop on our way to the store but it should only take a few minutes."

"All right. I'm not in a hurry. I told Yvonne I'd be back around six."

"What are y'all going to see?"

"We don't even know yet."

"You make it official yet?"

"Naw, we're just really good friends."

"C, man, please stop fronting. You know you caught some feelings."

I finally admitted it. "Yeah... I did."

"Finally! I'm happy you decided to be real with yourself. Listen, I'll be right back. I gotta pick this up right quick."

As we pulled in the driveway, I couldn't help but notice that big blue Audi A8. "Hey Mark, isn't that your friend Big Mike's car?"

"Yeah."

"I thought you weren't going to mess around with that guy because he's dangerous."

"No, *you* said you weren't going to mess with Big Mike. He's cool with me. Here, listen to this song and I'll be right back."

While waiting for Mark, I turned down the music and called my grandmother, but she wasn't home. I fidgeted around a bit, feeling strange and kind of nervous.

Finally, Mark came back and told me to pop the trunk.

"What took you so long, man?" I asked.

"I was taking care of some business."

"What kind of business?"

He pointed at me and winked.
"That's nunya business."

"Man, I thought we were better than this. What happened to being real with each other?"

"We can, Caleb. We'll talk about it all later."

"Yeah, that's fine. Just turn up the music. And I need the name of this playlist, so I can follow it."

The song's bass made his speaker vibrate. We rode in silence for a couple of blocks, nodding our heads in unison. Then, I heard a police squad car blasting their siren behind us. Mark pulled over and we waited patiently to see what was going on. The officers had a K-9 unit for backup. As they approached the car, the dogs began barking and jumping uncontrollably. I cringed, looking over to see a frantic look on Mark's face.

Chapter Twelve

"Why are they messing with me? I haven't done anything," Mark asked.

The officers reached the car and Mark rolled down the window. The dogs continued to bark ferociously.

"Can I see your license and proof of insurance?" The officer peered into the car.

"Yes, sir." Mark reached into his back pocket.

By then, the dogs were barking even louder and jumping up and down on the side of the car.

The officer scanned the items before peering back into the car. "Dogs are pretty excited. You boys wouldn't happen to have something in this car that you shouldn't have?"

I looked at Mark and he said, "No."

"Can you boys step out of the vehicle?"

As I stepped out of the car, I remembered a line from a rap song saying police officers can't search your car without a warrant. I didn't dare say a word, though. My hands were shaking like crazy as I put two and two together. We were going to have to do some serious explaining to these officers.

As we waited on the sidewalk, the officers searched the car and opened the trunk. "My, my, my... what do we have here? Whose dope is this, boys?"

Forget explaining. I had a date at six. "Not mine, officer. Can I call my grandmother?"

"No. Whose drugs are these?" "I don't know, sir," Mark said.

"I guess we're taking both of you in, then."

I was not about to get caught up in something illegal for Mark again. "Officer, my name is Caleb Farnsley. I live with my Grandmother, Lois. I was just riding with Mark. I don't know anything about what you found."

"Yeah, yeah, yeah. You both are looking at three to five years in prison if you don't cooperate with us. So, I'll ask you again. Whose drugs are these? Otherwise, you boys might as well kiss your freedom goodbye."

"No, officer. Please don't take me to jail. It's not mine." I looked over at Mark, pleading. "Tell them, Mark."

Mark shrugged. "Not mine, either."

"All right, that's it. Both of you are under arrest." We were handcuffed, read our Miranda rights, and led to the squad car.

Not again! This cannot be happening to me all over again, I thought.

"Please sir, I didn't do anything." I begged the officer, trying to be heard over the barking dogs.

Mark kept his eyes straight ahead and didn't say a word.

"Man, tell them Mark. You know I didn't have anything to do with this. I was just riding with you."

Mark remained silent and they took both of us in. All I could think about was how I was going to explain this to my grandmother. This would be the second time I stood Yvonne up, fooling with Mark. It was a short ride to the station in the cruiser, but each passing second seemed like an eternity. When we arrived, they took my mug shot, fingerprints, and shoestrings. Then they placed us in a holding cell.

I was so livid, I couldn't even look at Mark. For years, we'd been friends and I'd given our friendship everything I had. If I was good, I made sure he was good. I always looked out for him and protected him. I would have never guessed he would have put me in that kind of jeopardy with the law *twice*, without any thought. It was utterly disappointing.

At least I know who my real friends are now, I thought as I leaned my head against the wall.

About ten minutes later, I found the courage to start praying. "Lord, please help me get me out of this mess. Please, Father, you know I didn't do anything. I thank you, Lord, for Who You are. You are my Rock, my Shield, and my Protector. You said no weapon formed against me shall prosper. I am innocent, and I know I'll get out of here. Please have mercy on me and allow me to learn a valuable lesson from all of this. In Jesus's name, Amen."

One of the officers let me out to make a phone call. I got very nervous because I didn't know what to say to my grandmother, but something inside me told me to hurry and call because the truth would set me free.

"Hello. Will you accept a collect call from an inmate at Cuyahoga County jail?" the telephone operator asked.

"Yes. Hello, who is this?"
"It's... it's... it's me,
Grandma."

"No.... Caleb?!"

"Yes, Grandma. Let me explain."
"Boy, you have done enough explaining. I'm so tired of you not listening to me. Haven't I told you to be aware of your surroundings at all times?"

"Yes, Grandma, but I didn't do anything this time."

"And what is this I hear? You and Mark had drugs in the car?"

How in the world did she always end up finding everything out before I could even tell her? Grandma had her ear to the streets! I thought, bewildered.

"Please, Grandma. Just hear me out. They were not mine. I was just riding with Mark to look for an outfit for prom when he decided to make a stop. When he came back, I noticed he put something in the trunk. Then we took off. While we were on the road, the police pulled us over because of the loud music. They opened the trunk and found drugs in Mark's car. It's like we were being set up or something."

"Caleb, are you sure they are Mark's drugs?" "I don't think so and personally, I don't even

care! I don't want to be involved in this mess at all."

"Caleb, you know I believe you're innocent. But don't speak to anyone without an attorney present. I've called your Uncle Cal and we will get you home."

"Okay. Please, Grandma. Please get me outta here."

"We will. Just be patient. Keep the faith. You'll be home before you know it."

"You have one minute before disconnection," the operator warned.

"Grandma, please call Yvonne and tell her what happened so she'll know I didn't stand her up. Hello? Hello?"

I walked back to the jail cell, relieved that Grams was working on my release. Two of the most excruciating hours passed by. Suddenly, I couldn't take it anymore. I cried out to God with all my heart and soul. "Lord, please have mercy on me! I know I don't deserve it, but I believe you will cover me."

"Shut up!" I could hear some of the other occupants scream out from their cells, but I didn't care.

"Please, Lord! Have mercy on me and get me out of here. Please, Lord. Hear my cry. I am not ashamed to call on your Holy Name, Lord. I need you to help me, Lord."

Finally, after two more hours, one of the officers came by my cell to tell me the news.

"Caleb Farnsley, you weren't charged with anything. You're very lucky. Under normal circumstances, you would have been charged by affiliation. They haven't set a bond for you or made anything official so just be patient."

"With all due respect, officer, I don't have a choice. I am sitting here in jail."

He smiled. "I'll monitor the situation and keep you posted."

"Thank you. About what time is it, officer?"

"It's almost eight."

"Man, I have been in here for almost four hours. I need my grandma to hurry and come get me outta this place."

I looked over at Mark, who was fast asleep on the cot. *How in the world can he sleep peacefully, knowing he got me into this situation? That's not a real friend. Thank You, God, for revealing that to me.*

While looking at the latest news magazine that the guard gave me, I drifted off to sleep and had a dream that angels and demons were fighting for my life. Revelations one and fourteen through fifteen says, "in the end, a man whose head and hair were white like white wool put a crown on my head. And his eyes were like a flame of fire. Even his feet were like burnished bronze."

When I turned around he said, "I will always be with you." Then he left.

"Caleb Farnsley? Your uncle has posted bail for you. You're still going to get a court date, depending on if your friend confesses. And we may need you as a witness for the investigation, so I would lay low if I were you."

"You've got it, officer. Right now, all I can say is, hallelujah. Praise God. I'm outta here." Shortly thereafter, they released me. I left without a backward glance at my fair-weather friend.

Uncle Cal and Grandma waited for me in the lobby. That's when I could no longer contain myself. As I got closer to them, tears of joy started running down my face.

"Come over here, boy, and give me a hug. I know God answers prayer, Caleb."

"Every time, Grams." I sniffed.

"It's all right, son. Go on and cry. You can mourn that relationship, because I know it meant a lot to you."

Uncle Cal patted me on the back. "Caleb, I know you're innocent, but you have to watch who you hang out with."

"You're dead on, Unc. I just thought Mark was my dude."

"Sometimes people are just associates. A real friend would never put you in that type situation – especially not twice."

"Right. But, even now, I still care about what happens to Mark. I forgive him and I'm praying for his salvation. Without it, he's headed down a very dark and dangerous path."

"Caleb, you are truly a real friend. Now tell me, who is Big Mike?"

"Be real, who in the world is your source, Grams? You're killing me. You always know what's going on."

"Don't change the subject, dear," she said as we walked out to Uncle Cal's car.

"He's a local drug dealer, about nineteen years old. Mark introduced me to him last month at a party. I had a bad feeling when I met him and the only conversation I had for him was about his car. He offered me a job making one thousand dollars a week, but I wasn't on it because I knew it was wrong."

"I'm so proud of you, Caleb. It's evident that you're thinking about what God would have you do before making decisions. That really shows that all that Bible study and praying has paid off for you. You're not just talking about it, you're being about it." I dapped Uncle Cal up inside the car.

I called Yvonne to fill her in as soon as I got to my room. She was so excited to hear from me, she started crying.

"Caleb Farnsley, I have been praying for you. I know you're innocent."

"Yes, I am. But I have a court date next week and I don't know what's going to happen."

"Nothing's going to happen. The Lord has it under control. Just continue to follow Him and He'll take care of you."

"Thanks, Yvonne. You always hold me down."

"Caleb, it's nothing. That's what I'm here for."

I heard a knock on my bedroom door. "Caleb, I would like to share something with you," my grandmother said. I told Yvonne I would call her back.

"Okay, come in," I called.

"Son, who you hang with is who you are. The people you spend the most time with leave some of their influence on you, whether good or bad. Let me give you an example. Your friend Yvonne is a Christian, she loves the Lord and speaks into your life, but Mark is the opposite. This is the second time you've been in trouble with him."

You don't even want to know about all the things we did before I moved in here, I thought to myself. "I know, Grandma. But he has been my friend for so many years."

"No Caleb. That's where you're wrong. A real friend wouldn't put you in danger."

"I hear you, Gram. From now on, I'll have to learn to keep a watchful eye."

"Listen, I'm not telling you something I heard. I'm telling you something I know."

"Yes, and I appreciate your wisdom. I just want to be successful in all areas of my life. I have graduation, work, and college to think about."

"To be successful, all you need are three things: the Father to shape you, the Son to mold you, and the Spirit to guide you."

"You're right. I am going to remember everything you've told me, so I can become a better person. I know I'm not perfect, but I will strive to be."

"Only Jesus is perfect, Caleb. You just do the best that you can and let the Lord do the rest."

"Speaking of rest, I am tired. I just want to shower, then crash."

She winked. "Me too. You know its waaaay past my bedtime."

"Sorry to have you out so late, Grams."

"Don't worry about it. That's what family

does. We help each other in all times of need."

Shortly after our talk, I jumped in the shower, then fell asleep. My bed felt like a big, luxury pillow compared to the flat, hard bunk at the county jail. Mark might still be there. He came from a single income household and I knew his mom was barely making ends meet. This was the last thing she needed.

That could have been me, out on my own and making poor choices. Boy, was I ever so thankful for my grandmother and uncle.

Grandma always said, "Be thankful for the little things, but strive for some big things."

Chapter Thirteen

Early the next morning, I woke up to the smell of bacon frying and the sound of gospel music playing.

Grandma and I said our "good mornings" and then she said, "I made some pancakes for you. Your plate is already made. It's sitting in the microwave. I also poured you a cup of orange juice. It's on the table."

"Wow, Grams. You are awesome. Here, let me fix your plate so we can eat together and serve one another."

"Now you're talking, and it sounds good to my ears."

I made her a cup of coffee with cream and sugar, just the way she liked it. As we sat at the table, I noticed Gram's mouth was twisted and her speech was slower than normal.

"Are you all right, Gram? You sound chopped and screwed," I joked.

She waved me off. "Boy, I'm fine." Then she tried to drink some of her coffee, but she couldn't lift the cup up to her mouth. That's when I knew something was wrong. I slowly walked her back to her room, then I ran to the phone to dial 9-1-1.

"Nine-one-one emergency. This is dispatcher, Lisa Longoria. What is your emergency?"

"I need help, please. My grandmother is not looking right."

"What are her symptoms?"

"All of a sudden her mouth twisted up and her speech became slurred."

"Sounds like she may have had a stroke. Where is she now?"

"She's lying down on the bed."

"Okay, just stay with her. I'm sending EMS over right now." She confirmed the address.

I hung up with the operator and went back to my grandmother's room. "Gram, it's all right. You're going to be fine."

"Son, there's nothing wrong with me, I'm just a little tired."

"Yes, there is something wrong and help is on the way. Please don't fight them once they get here."

About five minutes later, the paramedics arrived. Grandma was still conscious and trying to talk.

"What's your grandmother's name, young man?"

"Lois."

"Miss Lois, we're going to give you a little oxygen and take your blood pressure. It seems like you had a mild stroke. We're going to take you to the hospital, so they can conduct further testing."

"Sir, is it all right if I ride in the ambulance?" I asked the paramedic as I dialed Uncle Cal's cell phone.

"Sure, let's go."

In the ambulance, I held Grandma's hand while the paramedics did their job. I sat by her side, wondering why this was happening to her. I had just gotten out of jail the night before! *What's going on Lord? Please talk to me. I haven't done anything wrong. Lord, why are you punishing my grandmother for my mistakes? It seems like You are far away and don't care, but You said You'll never leave me or forsake me. So please, if You can hear me, help my grandma because she loves You.*

Finally, we reached the emergency room, where they gave Grandma some fluids and medicine. Then the doctor came out to talk to us.

"We're going to keep Lois overnight for observation. If the test results come back normal, she should be able to leave tomorrow."

"What happened, doctor?"

"Well, your grandmother had a mild ischemic stroke. Her blood pressure was elevated and we noticed a blood flow blockage on her stress test."

All the stress I've been causing her lately, I thought and lowered my head.

"Is she going to be all right?" Uncle Cal asked.

"Yes, I believe so. We gave her some blood thinners and, with some healthy changes like a healthy diet and exercising, she should be just fine."

"Thank you, doctor." I said, relieved.

He nodded. "And your name, young man?"

"Caleb Farnsley, and this is my Uncle Cal and his wife, Shirley."

"Nice to meet you all. Even under these circumstances, you seem like you're a very close and loving family. I'm Dr. Mackley."

"Thanks, Dr. Mackley."

"No problem. Just let her get some rest, take good care of her, and she should be back to herself soon. If you guys need anything, don't hesitate to call me."

I thanked him again. After we looked in on Grandma, Uncle Cal grabbed his car keys.

"Caleb, me and your Aunt Shirley are going to head home. Momma will be okay. Are you coming with us?"

"No, Uncle Cal. I'm going to stay here with her. After all she's done for me, it's my turn to be here for her."

"Okay, Caleb. Call me when you're ready and I'll come and take you home."

A few minutes later, Grandma was sound asleep, and I was sitting on the chair, watching TV. I text Yvonne and told her what happened. She told me to give Grandma a hug and kiss for her.

Shortly after, her nurse came in with a lunch tray. Although it looked good, I didn't have the least bit of an appetite.

After the day's events, I just sat quietly studying my grandmother's pretty face. I was hoping and praying she would make a full recovery. Suddenly, I became angry inside. I still didn't understand why bad things happened to good people: my mom, dad, me, and my grandmother.

"God, if You can hear me, then please say something. I am going to go on a holy hunger strike until You speak to me because I can't see You, hear You or feel You. What are You doing in my life? Do You really love me? Is this how You show me?"

It was almost eleven at night and my eyes were getting heavy. I repositioned myself in the chair and drifted off to sleep. I had a vision of the same person as before, the man whose head and hair were like white wool and whose eyes were like James of fire, just like in Revelations, 1:14.

He walked up to me from a distance and said, "Caleb Farnsley, every breath you take, every step you make, My eyes are on you. Do you know Who I am? I am the Alpha and the Omega, the Beginning and End. I have shed My own blood for your sake. I told you I would never leave you nor forsake you. I am the Lord of lords and King of kings. But you still have doubt. Listen carefully, My Father gave you to me a long time ago. Caleb, I knew you before you were born.

"You've asked what I am doing in your life. How selective your memory is, Caleb. Right now you're going through a test. I know you share the same faith that fills your grandmother and your mother Eunice, and I know the same faith continues strong in you. When your faith remains strong through many trials, it will bring you much praise and glory and honor on the day when I am revealed to the whole world. So, this is what I want you to do. Remain in Me and I will remain in you. Apart from Me, you can do nothing. Love others as you love yourself. Always help anyone who is in need. By doing this, My Father may leave you a blessing. And last but not least, tell others about Me. I can save them. You remember, you have prayed to Me about your friend Mark. Tell him he's forgiven. Even though he doesn't know Me yet, it is because of you. I have gotta go. I love you.

"Oh, oh... I almost forgot. Lois will be back on her feet in a few days. She and I go way back. We've been talking every day for the past fifty-seven years and she is beyond faithful. Caleb, always listen to her. Continue to be obedient and know I am with you always, even to the end of the age."

"Caleb... Caleb?"
"Huh?"

Grandma's voice was strained and raspy. "Wake up. Your uncle called. He's on his way to get you."

After giving Grandma a goodnight kiss, I headed down to the lobby and waited for Uncle Cal. I felt confident that she was going to be just fine. Jesus' comforting words left my soul aglow and I was walking on cloud nine. I was full of joy because I had heard the voice of Jesus and I knew my life would never be the same.

Epilogue, the year 2023

Four years later, I'm a graduate of Ohio State University and am currently enrolled at Case Western Reserve University School of Medicine. One day, I will be known as Doctor Caleb Farnsley, with my own private practice specializing in cardiology. My beautiful wife of two years, Yvonne Farnsley, is a social worker. She loves the Lord with her whole soul and her actions consistently show it. She is currently pregnant with our first child. We're expecting a healthy baby boy.

After graduating high school, I lost touch with Mark. I tried reaching out to him when I came home during the first college break, but he was still caught up in drama with George, Pete, and Big Mike. From that point on, I realized he was never going to learn. I kept my distance from him, but continued to pray for his salvation.

You could say all my dreams have finally come true. My grandmother was the loudest one at both my high school and college graduations. She went home to be with the Lord at the end of last year. Although it hurt me to lose her at first, I was okay with it because she was ready. I've never seen someone so prepared and excited to meet the Lord.

I will make sure her legacy reaches generation after generation within our family. Not just with her recipes, sayings, and old traditions, but with a true shared love for God and people. Grandma Lois loved hard and she loved unconditionally. Her words of wisdom and loving kindness have shaped me into the man I am today.

I'm looking forward to the bright future that's ahead of me. I know I owe it all to God first, then to my parents, and last but not least, to my beautiful grandmother, Lois. As Yvonne and I raise the children that will come from our union, I will always remember to teach them love, dignity, and respect for self and others. That's how I know I will never forget what Grandma said.

Whoever denies the Son does not have the Father, the one who confesses the Son has the Father also. 1st John 2:23 NASB

Made in the USA
Lexington, KY
19 November 2018